Born in New York in 1912, Elliott Arnold was a reporter for the *Brooklyn Times* and the *New York World-Telegram* from 1929 to 1942. He enlisted in the Army in June 1942, served in North Africa, Italy and the South Pacific, and was discharged, as captain in the Air Force, in October 1945. He received the Bronze Star from General MacArthur.

Mr. Arnold is author of many books, including the following novels: TWO LOVES, PERSONAL COMBAT, ONLY THE YOUNG, THE COMMANDOS, TOMORROW WILL SING, BLOOD BROTHER, EVERYBODY SLEPT HERE, WALK WITH THE DEVIL and THE TIME OF THE GRINGO.

BLOOD BROTHER, Mr. Arnold's celebrated novel about Chief Cochise and Tom Jeffords, is the story from which the movie *Broken Arrow* was made. Using the film title, Mr. Arnold has now written, in BROKEN ARROW, a book primarily for younger readers and containing much of the material and story of BLOOD BROTHER.

Broken Arrow

Broken Arrow

by ELLIOTT ARNOLD

With Illustrations by Frank Nicholas

DUELL, SLOAN AND PEARCE • NEW YORK

LITTLE, BROWN AND COMPANY • BOSTON

DUELL, SLOAN AND PEARCE–LITTLE, BROWN
BOOKS ARE PUBLISHED BY
LITTLE, BROWN AND COMPANY
IN ASSOCIATION WITH
DUELL, SLOAN & PEARCE, INC.

Published simultaneously in Canada
by Little, Brown & Company (Canada) Limited

PRINTED IN THE UNITED STATES OF AMERICA

For my son, Tommy,
and for all boys and girls,

so that they may know that with good will and with understanding, all hatreds may be ended, and all men — of all races and colors and religions — can break the arrow of war and live with each other as brothers, in peace.

AUTHOR'S NOTE

This book was written in response to many requests that I abstract from my novel *Blood Brother* the essential story of the historic friendship of Tom Jeffords and the Apache Chief, Cochise, and present it in a less complicated form for younger readers. I should like to express my thanks to Twentieth Century-Fox Film Corporation for permission to use for a title *Broken Arrow*, the name of the film which was made from *Blood Brother*.

Broken Arrow

CHAPTER I

Tahzay, son of Cochise, lay flat on the sun-baked earth and squinted down the long corridor leading up to the narrow entrance to the East Stronghold of the Chiricahua Apaches in the Dragoon Mountains. For many days Tahzay had come there to wait with the sentry for the return of Cochise from the raid in Mexico. Suddenly he stiffened and he asked with excitement: "Is that dust? Are they coming?"

The sentry, leaning on a long rifle, looked down at the eager boy and grunted. "It is dust, but it is made by the wind and not by the hoofs of horses. If you hope to become a warrior, Tahzay, and serve your father, you will have to sharpen your eyes."

Tahzay looked up. "I will be a warrior. Maybe I will be chief."

"Maybe," the sentry said. "If you are a great warrior."

It was late fall, the time the Chiricahua Apaches called "Earth Is Reddish Brown." The early afternoon sun was very hot. Without taking his eyes away from the trail, Tahzay asked: "When will my father take me out with his warriors?"

The sentry shifted his position and again looked down at the son of the chief of the Chiricahuas. He saw a boy already tall for his age, as Cochise himself was tall among other Apaches. He saw a strong, broad-shouldered body, muscled by the vigorous training given to all Apache boys. The sentry thought: This one truly is the son of Cochise.

"How old are you, Tahzay?" the sentry asked.

"I have almost eleven harvests," the boy replied.

"That old? Are you certain? You do not lie? Your father would punish you for the smallest lie."

"I do not lie," Tahzay said. "I have passed the tenth birthday."

"It did not seem that long," the sentry said. "Then you do not have long to wait. One of these days Cochise will take you with him on a raid in Mexico and then we all will see what kind of blood flows in your body."

Tahzay raised his head and looked steadily at the sentry. "It is the blood of Cochise," he said.

The sentry looked down at the stern, childish face.

"There is no doubt of it," he said at last. Then he lifted his head. His body tensed. He pointed a bony arm: "THERE! *There!* There they come! And he rides at the head!"

Tahzay leaped to his feet. He trembled. He shaded his eyes with his hand. Below, in the valley, he could make out

[4]

the column of men and horses. He whirled and raced back into the Stronghold. "They come!" he shouted. "And Cochise rides at their head!"

Just then the sentry fired a shot into the air. From the valley came answering shots. The music makers in the camp pounded their drums. Women began to sing. The holy shamans began to chant sacred verses.

Then the returning warriors filed through the narrow opening into the Stronghold. They kicked their weary ponies into action and shouted.

The women screamed: "Here they come, and he rides before them!"

Children clapped their hands and danced and dashed up to the returning warriors, who scooped them up and sat them on the necks of the ponies. Tahzay stood at the side of his mother, Tesalbestinay. More than anything else in the world he would have loved to have run up to his father, to be lifted onto his horse, but he now was almost eleven and he thought it would be without dignity. Instead he stood erect and looked upon his father and he thought his heart would beat itself out of his body.

It was the last great raid of the season, before Ghost Face would come upon the land and lock the high mountains in snow and cold. There were more than a hundred Apache warriors. With them were captured Mexican women and children, horses and mules.

The eyes of every person in the great clearing in the Stronghold centered on the man leading the warriors. They chanted his name: "Cochise! Cochise! Cochise!"

Cochise rode proudly, his shoulders squared. He guided his horse with his knees. He held a long lance in one hand. Eagle feathers fluttered at the end of the lance. In his other hand he held a shining double-barreled shotgun.

His face was narrow and stern. His eyes were large. His nose was sharp and jutted arrogantly. The sun was full on him, showing the remains of the red and black streaks of paint on his face, showing the thick, black hair held in place with a band around his forehead. The year was 1855 and Cochise was forty years old.

As the men filled the clearing, women searched among them to see who was missing. As each woman recognized her own man her voice lifted more strongly. When all the warriors were gathered the eyes of some women still searched but they could not see their men.

The warriors remained in their saddles. Then Nahilzay, chief war lieutenant to Cochise, raised his spear for silence. His eyes glittered as he looked upon Cochise, whom he worshipped above all men. When Cochise nodded his head, Nahilzay announced in a loud voice the names of the men who had been killed on the raid.

Upon hearing the names, which numbered fourteen, the women of these slain men cried out, and then took their children with them and went to their wickiups. There they took off their gay clothing and cut their hair. They put black shawls on their heads and went to a far side of the Stronghold and sang a bitter song.

Meanwhile all the warriors except Cochise dismounted. Cochise ordered that all the booty brought back on the captured animals be piled up in the clearing. Cochise looked upon his people. He raised his right hand. "Nochalo will make a ceremony," he said. His voice was low and penetrating. "There are many horses. Many mules. Many guns. There is maize. There are blankets — good blankets of the Mexican soldiers. There are children of the Mexicans to the number of seven and Mexican women to become wives to Apaches. White Painted Lady rode with her Sons of the Woods. Nochalo will make a ceremony."

Cochise dismounted and handed the reins to Tesalbestinay. He looked down at Tahzay. It was with the greatest of difficulty that the boy restrained himself from flinging his arms around his father. Cochise rested his hand for a moment on Tahzay's shoulder. The boy quivered with pleasure.

Then, as the sun rested for a moment on the western rim of the Stronghold, Cochise began to distribute the booty taken in Mexico. He called out the name of Nahilzay, and when that warrior, his eyes filled with devotion, stepped before him, he bade him take what he needed from the pile. When Nahilzay made his selection and stepped back, Cochise called the name of Skinyea, and then of Pionsenay. One after the other, the fighting men took what they needed.

As Cochise distributed the spoils, with Tahzay standing straight and proud at his side, the women again began to sing; and as the name of each warrior was called out by Cochise, that name was included in the singing and the man was praised to the heavens. And Tahzay tingled and

[7]

thought how he would feel when his own name would one day be so lauded.

When each warrior had received his share, Cochise gave out things to women who had no men, to old men too feeble to fight. To the poorest he gave the most. He set aside things for the women who had left to mourn their dead.

After the last of the plunder was given away — except for what Cochise kept for his own family needs — the seven Mexican children were led forth. Tahzay looked at them as they shivered and quaked, clinging to each other for support. He thought they looked skinny and weak next to Apache children. Soon, he thought, they would be as deep-chested and strong as the children in the families of the Apaches who would adopt them.

The people left the meeting place and went to their wickiups to prepare for the evening festivities. Presently in the clearing there were only Tahzay and Cochise, and Cochise's two brothers, Juan and Naretena. Juan was a big, burly warrior. He said to Naretena: "You should have been there!" Shaking his head, living again the excitement of the raid, Juan strode off, bearing his share of the booty.

Naretena watched him depart. Naretena was thin and sickly. He was no warrior and he had no wife. It was said he had worms in his lungs which made him cough blood. Although he did none of the things the Apaches considered manly, Naretena was a man of great intelligence, and Cochise respected him and sought his counsel and listened to his advice.

Now Cochise said: "We will talk. Come to my wickiup." Then Cochise looked at Tahzay. "Come with us, my son," he said. "You are becoming a man and you should know about things."

The two men and the boy walked to Cochise's wickiup and entered. It was a round, dome-shaped dwelling, made of poles covered with skins. The men seated themselves and Tahzay squatted at the side of his father. Never before had Cochise permitted him to attend serious meetings with other men. For a little while the two brothers looked at each other in courteous silence.

At last Naretena said: "I have seen Americans."

Cochise's eyes flickered. "Where?"

"Tucson. There are new people in Tucson. The ownership is changed."

"What ownership?" Cochise asked arrogantly.

"Americans now own the land south of the Gila River," Naretena said. "The border is changed. We now are in the country of the Americans. There will be American soldiers and American forts. Many Americans will come and raise cattle and dig in the ground for yellow and white iron."

The flow of words brought on a coughing spell. Cochise sat in silence, making no comment. When Naretena finished coughing, he continued.

"When the war between the Americans and Mexicans was over it was not settled between them which land belonged to Americans and which belonged to Mexicans. Many Americans came from the direction of the rising sun. There was much talk. The Americans gave the Mexican chief, Santa Anna, yellow iron. Now the land from the Gila down belongs to Americans. We live in America."

For a long time Cochise did not reply. Tahzay watched his father's face grow harsh. He did not understand too much of what his uncle had said but he saw that it had displeased his father.

"Settled between Americans and Mexicans!" Cochise said finally. "No Indians were asked! Yellow iron was given and the line of the earth was changed and the Mexicans and the Americans are satisfied. But we have lived here for many harvests. This is the country of the Apache. We were here before the Americans, and before the Mexicans. No one thought to settle with us!"

He controlled himself. His voice quieted. "They come with their guns and they drive away animals we need for food. They dig holes in the ground and they say we must change our old ways of living. They say we must live as they do. And they grow greater in numbers all the time. And we grow smaller and soon there may not be room for both of us." He raised his head proudly. "We are not a conquered people! No warriors have defeated us!"

"No one of the earth," Naretena agreed. "Yet our numbers do not increase. Now we are no more than twelve hundred. Three hundred fighting men. The white men are without number. They are as blades of grass."

Cochise lowered his head and stared moodily. "It is the closing time for us, maybe." The cool evening wind scratched on the skin of the wickiup. "We must walk the path of the white man."

Naretena nodded. *"Enju,"* he said, using the Apache word for "It is well."

"The Americans are warriors," Cochise mused. "They are brave. They fought the Mexicans and the sun set for the Mexicans here. It is afternoon for the Apaches, maybe. We must walk the white path. It has been in my mind for a long time. The white men know things and we must learn from them. If we do not the sun will set for us. We cannot destroy them. We can fight them, but ten grow where one is defeated. To live we must learn and change our ways. People before us have vanished because they could not learn how to make changes."

Naretena asked softly: "What of Mangas Coloradas?"

"We will have a big talk with Mangas Coloradas," Cochise replied. "His business is with his own people, the Mimbres Apaches. We will tell him what the Chiricahua Apaches will do."

As the last of the day's light scurried out of the Stronghold and the darkness of the hours of peace slipped in to take its place, the women worked hard and the men cleaned themselves and made ready for the celebration. Mules were butchered for the feast and set to roast over fires. The women prepared roasted mescal, cakes of mesquite bean and acorn, fruit of the giant cactus.

In the gathering darkness the fires glared and the wind rose and the music makers chanted and pounded on drums and played on fiddles and guitars.

Then the warriors arrived in the clearing. The fighting

men were bathed and they wore ceremonial dress, adorned with colored stones. The men gathered in a great circle. In one part of the circle, several blankets had been folded and set one on top of the other, to make a seat for Cochise.

The women formed another circle around the men's circle, and outside of it. The men and women swayed back and forth to the rhythm of the music and then they began to chant: "Here Cochise comes! Here Cochise comes!"

Cochise walked slowly to his place in the circle. At his side was Tahzay. Cochise wore his shirt of soft buckskin, painted with markings for the elements: Hail, Snow, Rain, Sunshine. Lightning blazed in a jagged streak across his chest. His arms were covered with leather and silver bands. Hanging from his right side was a leather pouch, containing two pieces of wood from a tree struck by Lightning. On his head was a red sash, holding two eagle feathers, one bright red, the other in its natural color. His face was newly painted, white and red.

As he stepped into his place in the circle, the sound of the chanting rose until it filled the great amphitheater: "His name is called! His name is called! Cochise! His name is called! Cochise! Cochise! Cochise!"

Cochise sat down on the folded blankets and gestured for Tahzay to sit next to him. This was the first victory ceremony Tahzay had ever been permitted to attend and he knew that his father must be thinking about starting him on the path to be a warrior. Tahzay took his place and tried to hold his face tight and hard and rigid as his father's.

Women dancers in elaborate buckskin robes burst into the cleared area and danced before Cochise, and then suddenly a man leaped into the clearing. The women vanished. The drums slowed down.

The man was Nochalo, chief medicine man to Cochise. He was small and wiry. His lower lip stuck out. His nose was long. He wore his holy shirt, marked not only with the elements, but with the symbols of the snake, the centipede, and the tarantula. In his hand was his medicine cord of four strands, with painted gourds at the end of each strand. He swung the cord in a great circle over his head and began the ritual of thanks for the success of the raid.

Slowly he lessened the whirling of the gourds until they fell upon his shoulders, and as the sacred number of four touched him he walked toward the direction of the rising sun.

Now Cochise turned to Tahzay and said to him in a low voice: "You should know what he is doing. This is an important ceremony. It has special meaning for us. We call all Indians 'People of the Woods.' But we have a special name for ourselves. Do you know what that name is, my son?"

"We are called 'Apache,' " Tahzay said.

"To the world we are Apaches," Cochise said. "But we do not call ourselves by that name in our ceremonies. Apache is a Pima Indian word and means 'enemy' in the Pima language. The Pimas called us Chiricahua Apaches, which means only 'Enemies from the Distant Mountains.'

But to us, in our hearts, we are 'Hiuah,' which means 'Men of the Rising Sun.' That is why Nochalo makes his first turn in that direction."

When he walked ten paces to the east, Nochalo paid his respect to the direction and then returned and walked ten paces north, returned, and then west and south. While he walked — his hands crossed on his chest, and the medicine cords dangling in front of him — he said nothing and there was no sound in the Stronghold except the low, slow beating of the drums and the murmur of the wind.

Nochalo now walked to Cochise. From a small leather pouch he took out a handful of tule pollen. He sprinkled a little of the pollen on the right foot of Cochise. He made a cross with the pollen on Cochise's forehead. Then he sprinkled his left shoulder, his left knee and his left foot. Then Nochalo returned to the clearing and chanted his thanks, reminding his Power that Cochise again was anointed with the symbol of Life. He directed his Power to permit the Chiricahua leader to remain long with his people and to continue his record of success against his enemies.

Now the dancers returned and as they danced the men ate and drank and sang of their experiences under the leadership of Cochise. Tahzay, at the side of his father, listened and thought that on the earth there could be no man as great as Cochise.

It was long after midnight and the moon was high when Nochalo again leaped into the clearing and cried: *"Cochise! they say to you: You! You! They call you again and again!"*

Cochise rose slowly and stepped before the fire. His lean

face was taut with pride. The firelight made shadows in the hollows of his cheeks. His body tensed. His eyes narrowed. His head jerked forward and he stared into the darkness. He held his right hand over his eyes, as though he were shielding them, and the people leaned forward as he started the pantomime of the raid.

As the people watched they could imagine him flat on the ground and they could make out the Mexican village and through his eyes they could see the people in the village and they could see the corrals filled with mules and horses. They could see Cochise giving the final instructions to his men, and then they could see the men breaking up into smaller groups and taking their places at the attack points. They could see each man inspect his weapons, and their throats were dry as they waited for Cochise to give the call for the attack.

Then the signal was given and the people sighed and they could see the warriors making their lightning thrusts from a dozen different places, on corrals, on houses, striking first here and then there, confusing the Mexicans who never knew from what direction the next assault would come.

Now, as Cochise acted out the raid, the people saw the warriors gathering horses and mules and starting back with them, as other warriors took weapons and clothing, and still others continued to race around, screaming, firing guns, loosing arrows. Captives were taken. And then, as suddenly as they attacked, the Apaches vanished.

Throughout the pantomime the people listened with a kind of quiet frenzy. Their eyes flashed and their fists clenched as the warriors who had been there relived the raid. Throughout his enactment, Cochise indicated very little of his own personal part in the attack. When he finished he walked abruptly away from the clearing and resumed his seat, his face again frozen into immobility.

Tahzay's eyes were sparkling. How long would it be, he thought, before he would know of these things himself?

Then the call was made for Nahilzay. The white teeth of the war lieutenant flashed as he leaped gracefully into the clearing. He began his account, his eyes on Cochise. He described how he had led a party of warriors to a corral and how his horse had been shot from under him and how he had been thrown from the horse directly in the line of the Mexican fire. He related that his danger was so great that he did not call upon anyone to help him, because anyone so called would be bound to come to him and he did not want to bring death to anyone. And then — he continued — Cochise, unbidden, had galloped across the clear field and had ridden to his side and had picked him up and, holding him shielded by his horse, had raced away to safety.

The women screamed: "Yieeeeeah! Yieeeeeah!" Cochise remained unmoved.

Then the small Skinyea, whose name meant "Canyon," took up the story and told how the men had regathered when the raid was over and how, soon afterward, they had heard the horses of the Mexican Rurales. The Chiricahuas divided into two bands. One band had continued on and the other, led by Cochise, assisted personally by Skinyea — who strutted cockily as he came to this part of the story —

remained hidden. They permitted the Mexican police to pass them by and then they attacked the Rurales from the rear and at the same time the Apaches who had gone on ahead turned around and attacked from the front. Caught between two grinding forces, the Rurales broke up and fled.

Pionsenay, whose name meant "Horse," came next. Then Juan, and then others, and so the stories were told through the night and the men listened and the women shrieked their birdlike cries of approbation and the dancers worked themselves into lathers and the singers became hoarse.

Finally, Holos, the Sun, lifted his red eye over the east rim of the Stronghold. The men stood up wearily and went to their wickiups to sleep. Cochise and Tahzay were the last to leave.

Tahzay, who never before had remained up through a night, watched his father stand straight and untired and lift his long arms to the new sun. And then he followed as Cochise walked toward their dwelling.

CHAPTER II

Toward the close of the winter in the beginning of the next year, just before Ghost Face made way for early spring, called "Little Eagles," the powerful Mimbres Apache chieftain, Mangas Coloradas, brought his leading warriors to the Stronghold, in response to an invitation from Cochise.

Mangas Coloradas was an older man than Cochise, and many Apaches in the different tribes considered him the leading Apache statesman, although it was acknowledged by all that he was not the equal of Cochise in military affairs. He was a man of imposing appearance. He was a larger man than even Cochise, and his largeness was everywhere on him. His body was huge, his arms and legs were bulky, his head was enormous. He had penetrating eyes. His nose alone was small — narrow, and almost delicate — and it gave his face the appearance of a wise owl.

Mangas Coloradas was Cochise's close friend and his sister was Tesalbestinay, wife of Cochise.

As the warriors of both the Chiricahua and the Mimbres tribes gathered for the meeting, Cochise said to Tahzay: "Men do not do things by themselves. When big decisions must be made it is well that men who are friends to each other talk about it first, so that the decision of one man does not hurt a friend. Come with me to this conference and listen well and remember what you see and hear."

The shamans from both tribes finished their religious rituals. The warriors squatted before the fires, their blankets wrapped around them. When the last of the reverences were made, Nochalo said: "Keep closed the cloud. Keep the black cloud closed. Cochise is outside the black cloud. Do not open its door."

The seated men muttered: *"Enju."* The conference was considered well-favored. Though a winter wind raced through the Stronghold, no branch had fallen from any tree. No owl had hooted, which would have been a bad sign.

Cochise began to speak. He said: "Are we not native to the earth around us? Are we not of the mountains, the air, the forest? Are not the deer and the mountain sheep part of our lives? Do not the birds sing for the Apache? Are the deer not grazing in our country? Are not the mountain sheep treading lightly on our rocks? Do not the shadows of the great eagles move upon our earth? Do not the cattle of the white men feed upon grass that grows upon the soil of the Apache? Do not the bodies of our fathers and of their fathers lie beneath the earth that belongs to the Apache? Is not the stream that runs on our earth for the slaking of our thirst? Why then do the white men come here? Why do they drive away our food? Why do they change our earth so that the Apache cannot live on it as before?"

His voice was hushed and yet it reached the ears of the farthest man. He paused and then he reviewed the history of the traditional enmity between the Indians and the Mexicans, going back to the days of the Spanish Conquistadores.

"Now there are new white men who come to our country," he said. "They are different from the Mexicans. They were at war with the Mexicans and they welcomed us when we joined them in their war. Then they made their peace with the Mexicans and now they no longer are enemies of our enemies. This land where we live, these mountains, these valleys, these animals, these birds, the wind and the rain and the snow and the hail, all of these things have belonged to the Apache. Yet for a long while the Mexicans said it belonged to them. And now the Americans have bought it and they now say it belongs to them."

He raised his head and looked around the natural majesty of the Stronghold. He said bitterly: "As though this earth can be traded like a horse!"

He continued: "Apaches fight Mexicans. Americans get killed in the fighting, because when a man has blood in his heart he does not pause to reflect, but he kills. And the slaying of Americans becomes a crime because this is now American country — so they say. And the Americans kill Apaches and there is no peace between us. Our people and the Americans no longer are brothers. The Americans are brave men. There are many more where they came from. More than all the Indians, it is said. Their soldiers soon will come to Tucson."

There was no sound from his listeners, who might have been the rocks themselves in the wavering light from the fire. Mangas Coloradas, looking at them, thought they were in a trance. No man could put men under a spell with words as could Cochise, he said to himself.

Cochise said: "When the great wind strikes a tree with enough force the tree must bend or else it will break." He looked slowly at the men around him. "So now I think it is time for the Chiricahuas to make peace with the white men, to go among them and live with them as brothers, to learn their ways and to make those ways into our ways to bring strength and wisdom to my people."

There was a long sigh from the warriors. Tahzay shivered. To make friends with white men! To live among them!

Mangas Coloradas cleared his throat. His voice was deep and rumbling. "My brother speaks with wisdom," he said. Then, in a leisurely manner, he told the old story of how Juan José, the last chief of all the Apache tribes, had been assassinated by white men he had befriended. "I have lived closely with these Americans in my own country," Mangas Coloradas went on. "I have studied their ways. Many of them speak with the forked tongue. First they warred with Mexicans and now they are at peace, as you have said. That is all right. But they say we too must be at peace with Mexicans even though the Mexican government still offers money for Apache scalps. The Americans should make laws for themselves and for people they have conquered — and not for us."

The listeners grunted their approval.

Cochise replied: "A man does not always do the things he wants to do. I do not explain the ways of the Americans. I do not think about them. I think of my own people. I think of the children of my people and the children who will come from those children. The Americans are here. They will not be driven away. I have led my people in war — but now I say that the Americans grow stronger while we grow weaker.

"They have guns which are better than our guns and our arrows and our spears. They are strange to our country and now they fight the country as well as us, but soon they will learn to make friends with the country and to use it as we do. They are brave men."

Cochise's voice filled with deep respect. Two things he respected more than anything else in men: one was truth and the other was bravery.

Mangas Coloradas said: "But the Americans do not have faith in the word of the Apache. They will not believe my brother is speaking the truth when he comes to them."

Cochise's eyes blazed. "No one has ever accused me of speaking with a crooked tongue!" he said in a deadly voice. "I have done many bad things, some of them so bad that Ghosts come to me in the night and swim in my head until it rocks. But I have never spoken a lie!"

"It is true," Mangas Coloradas agreed. "Truth has a value among all our people but in none of us has it so great a value as with my brother. But do the Americans know this?"

Cochise was unable to answer immediately. The thought of lying was so abhorrent to him he felt a physical nausea. Then he said: "Every man knows this."

The discussion was taken up by other warriors, and finally one Chiricahua Apache, who was not yet recognized as a prominent fighter, a man named Gokliya, spoke up: "One does not question the wisdom of Cochise. Still, some things are right for some men and wrong for others. For so long as the memory of our people goes, we have lived by our bravery and our wits." His voice was sly. "It is not the Apache way to live like women, to grow things from the ground, to be grandmothers to cattle. Our people would grow soft with such a life. Our enemies would rise and destroy us."

"The Americans are not soft nor womanly," Cochise replied. "To learn their ways does not mean to become blind and deaf." Now Cochise stood up. "Listen to me, all men. I speak to my own Chiricahuas. I speak openly so that Mangas Coloradas and his warriors will know what I do. I will make peace with the Americans. For those who stay with me — it will be as I command. If the Chiricahua people do not want to stay with me, there are other leaders they may choose. I know in my heart what is right for my people. I want all my people to follow me. But those who follow me must walk with me with their hearts as well as with their words.

"I will go to the Americans and tell them what I have decided. When I tell the Americans my people want peace I shall be speaking for all the people who walk with me. But it will be my word that I give. I will guarantee that word."

He looked gravely at the men seated around him.

"Leave me now if my path displeases you," he said slowly. "That is your right. But those who stay with me will do as I pledge." He paused and then he said: "After I give my word, all who remain will be bound by that word, and any man who does a bad thing and violates my word — I myself will kill."

Now he faced Mangas Coloradas, who had listened to his talk with a solemn face. Cochise said: "This is Chiricahua country. When I make this peace it means that the land of the Chiricahuas is peaceful land. We have walked together. Now I take this path. I do not want to be your enemy. I love your people almost as much as I love my own. But I say to you that any Mimbres warrior who violates my word becomes my enemy. It is understood?"

Mangas Coloradas nodded his great head heavily. "It is understood."

Cochise said to his warriors: "Those of my people who do not want to follow me — walk away now!"

For a moment there was silence and then the man named Gokliya leaped to his feet. "I am an Apache and a warrior!" he shouted. "I do not become tame for the white eyes. I walk away!"

A few other men joined him and then Gokliya, his face twisted with rage, screamed: "I am ashamed of my Apache brothers! I am ashamed of the Apache name by which they know me. From now on I no longer am Gokliya. From now on I shall be known by the name Mexican enemies call me: Geronimo!"

CHAPTER III

In the early part of March of that year, the time the
Apaches called "Many Leaves," Cochise learned from his
spies that four companies of United States Dragoons had
occupied Tucson and that for the first time the flag of the
United States had been raised over the ancient walled Mexican settlement in the Santa Cruz Valley.

A few weeks later he was informed that the Dragoons
had continued south and had made temporary camp where
the headwaters of the Sonoita River joined the Santa Cruz
River, a section called Calabasas by the Mexicans, and that
army engineers were prospecting in the country, which was
about seventy miles from the Stronghold, for a permanent
site for a fort.

Cochise summoned to his wickiup Naretena, his brother,

and his chief lieutenant, Nahilzay, and he told them what he had learned.

"This is the time, maybe, to see the chief of the American soldiers and make a peace with him," Cochise said.

Nahilzay said immediately: "Let me go. It might be dangerous for the chief of the Chiricahua Apaches to put himself in the power of Americans."

"I do not believe that," Cochise said. "I believe I can treat with them in honor."

Nahilzay snorted contemptuously. "Honor! White man's honor!"

"White men have honor too," Cochise said.

Naretena spoke: "It is something only the chief may do. If there is to be a peace it must begin with trust."

Tahzay, squatting in a dark place in the wickiup, could not contain himself. Although he knew he should not interrupt the conversation of his elders, he cried: "Take me with you, Father."

Cochise turned his head and frowned. Then he said: "Come here, my son."

Tahzay, frightened at having interrupted his elders, came slowly to his father. Cochise looked at him for a long time and then he put his hand on his shoulder. "You have said a good thing," he said. "If things go as I plan them to go you will have much to do with Americans later on." He looked at Nahilzay. "This much do I believe in the honor of the Americans. I will go to see the American *nantan,* and I will take my son with me."

In a hidden place in the forest not far from where the American dragoons were encamped in the Sonoita Valley, the Indians halted. Nahilzay said: "I still do not trust white men. Let me go into the fort first — before you put yourself in their power."

"I will go," Cochise said.

Nahilzay said: "Why not send word to the American *nantan?* If he is as brave and as honorable as you believe he is, he will have no fear to come here to you."

Cochise thought for a moment. *"Enju.* I will do as you ask."

"I will go," Nahilzay said.

"You do not have any language but your own," Cochise said. "Pionsenay has some Spanish. He will go. Pionsenay, go to the camp of the Americans and give the word to the American *nantan* that I await him here and would speak to him to make a peace between our peoples."

Pionsenay disappeared among the trees.

"He will not come," Nahilzay said.

"I believe he will come," Cochise said.

They sat down and waited for more than an hour. This was farther away than Tahzay had ever been from the tribal land of his people. He sat close to his father, his arms around his knees. As they all waited Nahilzay became more and more restive. Again and again he cocked his head alertly, fearing they might be treacherously surrounded by enemy soldiers. Cochise sat quietly, his face impassive.

Another hour passed, and now Nahilzay was like a wild

animal. He pleaded with Cochise to leave before he was captured by soldiers. Cochise, who was telling Tahzay about different ways to hunt deer, ignored him. And then, as Nahilzay was again demanding that they leave, Pionsenay trotted up to them.

"The American *nantan,* Major Steen, awaits you nearby," Pionsenay said.

"How many soldiers has he with him?" Nahilzay demanded immediately.

"He is alone," Pionsenay said.

Cochise rose to his feet, a faint smile on his lips. "He is a brave man," he said.

Led by Pionsenay, Cochise walked through the forest to a small clearing where a short, wiry American major, with sparkling blue eyes, was waiting. Nahilzay looked around nervously in all directions. Cochise walked up to the captain and held up his hand in the sign of peace. Cochise said: "I am Cochise."

The major replied: "I am Major Enoch Steen."

The greetings were translated by a trembling Indian who stood at Steen's side.

Cochise studied the face of the American officer. "I come to talk peace for the Chiricahua Indians."

"Good. I have wanted to talk to the great chief of the Chiricahuas. I too want to talk peace." The words were translated rapidly. "But there is no need to talk in the forest like animals. Come to my camp and we can smoke and talk in comfort."

When these words were translated, Cochise's eyes

flickered with quick suspicion and Nahilzay stepped to his side, his hand gripping his gun. Cochise said: "There are many soldiers in your camp. Five bands of soldiers are away on scout, but there are still many left there."

Steen's eyes widened at this demonstration of the accuracy of Cochise's information about activities in the fort. He said: "I am here alone. I came alone when Cochise was standing among *his* warriors."

Cochise nodded. "I will go to your camp." Again Nahilzay protested. Cochise quieted him. He said: "I am no less brave than the *nantan* of the American soldiers." He fixed his eyes on Steen. "Your word that my people and I will be safe?"

Steen held out his hand. "I give you my word."

Cochise looked puzzled at the extended hand. Then he put out his own hand and the men touched their fingers.

The American soldiers gaped as the party rode into the camp. When the men reached Steen's headquarters, a soldier ran forward to take the major's horse. Steen ordered instantly: "Take the horse of the chief, Cochise."

Cochise leaped lightly from his horse and handed the reins to the soldier. The soldier walked away, muttering, "He acts like a general!"

When all the men were seated in Steen's office, Cochise looked around curiously. His eyes fell upon a large map tacked on the wall. "What is the picture writing?" Cochise asked.

Steen attempted to explain what a map was. The Indian who was translating fell down trying to change the English words into Apache. Steen showed Cochise where the Dragoon Mountains and the Chiricahua Mountains were located. The Apache's face again became suspicious and he exchanged a glance with Nahilzay.

The appearance of the heartland of the Chiricahua people on a sheet of paper had a profound effect on the Indians. The military markings were similar to the symbols on the sacred shirts of the medicine men and it seemed to the Indians that Steen must possess a power over the Chiricahua land because he had it on the paper.

"Is the method of preparing these things a secret?" Cochise asked at last.

"It requires instruction," Steen said.

"Can one learn? Might the land of our enemies be placed on paper for us?"

"It might be," Steen said. "If the Chiricahua people and the Americans were brothers."

Cochise stared for a long time at the map. He said: "I come for peace. The Chiricahuas have never looked upon the Americans as enemies. Only the Mexicans. Still there is bad blood between us and there is fighting. I come to put an end to the fighting and to say that the Chiricahuas and the Americans should live as brothers. The Americans know many things. I want the Chiricahuas to learn these things. In return for the learning I come to offer our mountains and our valleys for the yellow and white iron the

Americans value. The Americans raise cattle. The Chiricahuas will protect the cattle against bad Indians. The country of the Chiricahuas will be peaceful and quiet."

Steen replied: "The Americans do not want to take from the Chiricahuas their mountains and their valleys. There is room enough for all of us. The Americans who come for gold and silver will not disturb the Apaches. The Americans want to live at peace with all peoples. The Americans come with many things — with clothing and food and horses and cattle. They want to trade with the Apaches as they trade among themselves."

Cochise said: *"Enju."*

He stood up and walked over to the map. He studied it keenly for a few moments and then, with a grasp of its significance that startled Steen, he moved a bony finger over it. "My people live here," he said. "This is Chiricahua land. I have no control over here where the sun rises, nor here where the sun sets, nor here in the north, nor in Mexico. This Chiricahua country I do control, and my people will not war upon their American brothers. And my people too will see that bad Indians do not come into the Chiricahua country to make war."

"Your words warm my heart," Steen said. "It is planned by us before long to establish a stagecoach line across all of this part of the country and some of that line will pass through Chiricahua land, through what is known as Apache Pass. It makes me happy to be able to tell my government that the Chiricahua people are at peace. We would like to build a trading post in Apache Pass. This place will have many things to trade with the Indians."

Cochise said with great dignity: "The wagons and the trading post may come into Chiricahua country. My warriors will guard the pass and see that men who work there and who travel through it are safe." He paused. "But there is something else. I do not speak with two tongues. I keep nothing hidden. This peace is made only with Americans. We still war with Mexico."

Steen pursed his lips. "My country is at peace with Mexico."

"It is no matter to me with whom your country is at peace!" Cochise retorted proudly. "That is the right of your government, to make war or peace. But Apaches were at war with Mexicans long before the Americans came to this country. We will continue to be so. Mexicans still collect gold from their government for Apache scalps. Are these the people you would have me call brothers?"

As he spoke his voice grew harsh. Nahilzay began to tremble with anger.

Steen lowered his eyes. He said: "You speak to me in honesty. I speak to you in the same manner. When my government made peace with Mexico it was agreed we would try to prevent Indians from raiding below the border. You must know how my duty lies. I am bound in honor to obey the orders of my government."

"I like your words," Cochise said. "It is possible to keep a pledge when those who make it know in advance all the parts of the pledge." He smiled. "Your soldiers must obey orders. It is true. But in order to prevent Apaches from raiding in Mexico they must first find the Apaches."

Steen nodded. "We will leave it at that."

Later the men left the headquarters. Steen ordered that food and clothing and tobacco be given to the Indians. "Accept these as a present from my government to mark our peace," he said. He held out a military carbine to Tahzay. "To the son of Cochise I give this gun and I pray that he fire it only on animals for food and never on Americans who are his friends."

Tahzay's eyes sparkled. But before he could accept the present he looked at his father for permission. Cochise nodded. Tahzay took the carbine and held it tightly. It was his first man-sized weapon.

Cochise led his horse up to Steen and rubbed the neck of the beautiful animal. He handed the reins to the captain. "He will carry you always in safety," he said. Then he gravely handed Steen his lance, and his bow and quiver filled with arrows. "Whenever we meet the American *nantan* will need no more weapons than I bear on me now."

CHAPTER IV

Throughout the rest of that year and through the early months of 1857 American pioneers poured into the Southwest. Cochise removed his people from the Dragoon Mountains, where they had their most permanent dwellings, led them across the Sulphur Spring Valley to the Chiricahua Mountains, and he settled them close to the springs that made Apache Pass so important a place for travelers.

In the desert country trails were made from water hole to water hole and from the moment men began their day's journey their one thought was to reach water by nightfall. By a freak of nature, the ugly, frightening stretch of Apache Pass was granted constantly flowing water, making a stop there necessary.

The new life Cochise had ordered for his people was

received by them in various ways. The older people accepted it contentedly. Women built wickiups with greater care, knowing they would not have to abandon them at any time. The women, who did all the domestic work among the Apaches, applied themselves to the tanning of hides, the making of moccasins and leather bags and clothing. They wove baskets to hold the fruit they gathered.

The warriors, however, did not take as gracefully to their unemployment. From childhood on, the male Apache was trained for nothing but the hunt and the raid. Now many of them drank too much and quarreled among themselves. Raids were still made in Mexico, but these were planned so skillfully by Cochise there was no need to repeat them too often. There was much leisure time — and this time, Cochise ordered, could not be spent, as before, wandering around in search of parties of American prospectors.

Nahilzay brought reports of discontent among the young warriors to his chief, but Cochise replied firmly: "It does not worry me. These men are young and filled with fire. An eagle does not change his nature overnight. But soon they will forget the old days."

Nahilzay shook his head. "They hear stories about the success the one who calls himself Geronimo is having, and how the warriors of Mangas Coloradas grow rich with American loot. Even the *Tontos,* the ones called Fools, make successful attacks on white men."

Cochise said: "On the sides of mountains and in some caves there are marks of picture writing. They were made by an ancient people that vanished. Why did they vanish?

Because they could not change as times changed. They continued to live in their old way although all around them there was change. The Chiricahua people will not die off that way. I will not permit it."

Nahilzay shrugged. "These are deep thoughts. They are beyond my understanding and beyond the understanding of the men. The peace is kept only because you ordered it. No one understands. But they obey. But food is growing less. The game is fleeing because of the Americans. The herds no longer come to the old places."

"Then we will seek new places," Cochise said. "Gather the warriors. They grow fat from laziness. Organize a big hunt. Only one thing: be sure it is to the north."

"Why must it be to the north?"

"Mexico is south."

"I do not understand."

Cochise smiled. "Then listen to me. I have made peace with the Americans. One day, maybe, I will make peace with Mexicans."

Nahilzay was aghast. "Peace with Mexicans!"

Cochise nodded slowly. "We have the friendship of the Americans now — even though they know we continue to raid in Mexico. The American *nantan* has to accept that violation of American law, because he is not strong enough to stop us. But that will not be so always. The Americans come in great numbers. Soon there will be enough of them to insist that we obey all — *all* — the American laws. When that time comes the Chiricahua people will be out of the habit of going into Mexico, maybe."

[37]

Nahilzay looked at him slyly. "We may find food if we hunt north, it is true. But there is no clothing to the north. There are no blankets, no weapons, no horses or mules or sheep."

"We will get these things from the Americans."

"How?"

"As the Americans get them from each other — by buying them."

"Buying them with what?"

"We can find the yellow iron the Americans treasure so much. We can work. We can even raise cattle as Americans do."

"Raise cattle!" Nahilzay said with disgust.

Cochise smiled again. "There is another way, more to your liking, maybe. Wagons soon will pass through our country. We have promised to protect these wagons from bad Indians. The Americans will give presents for that."

"The warriors will refuse to act as grandmothers to Americans!"

"The warriors will not refuse to do anything I order them to do," Cochise said very quietly.

Nahilzay pondered over this and then he stretched out his arm and placed his hand on the shoulder of his leader. He said gravely: "No matter what path you lead, I follow. If it is my life that is needed, it belongs to you. But among us no man continues to be leader unless the people wish it so. If it is decided that some devil is twisting your mind so that you no longer are fit to lead them, they will choose another chief."

"Who dares speak of a devil in me?" Cochise demanded angrily.

Nahilzay now said slowly: "Geronimo spreads word that you have been bewitched."

Cochise recoiled as though he had been struck. It was believed by Apaches that some men were captured by dark forces. These men appeared to be the same as other men, but they were believed to be doomed.

Nahilzay spat. "May a coyote eat him!"

Cochise shuddered with rage. "Bring Gokliya here."

"He is in Mexico. He has twenty warriors who call him chief."

"Bring him here!"

"If he refuses to come?"

"There are men among us who seek a warpath."

"If he still refuses?"

"Give him my word. I will do him no harm."

When Cochise returned to his wickiup his wife Tesalbestinay was busy scraping flesh from deer hide to prepare it for tanning. Seated next to her, playing with sticks, was Cochise's younger son, Nachise, who was just two. At that moment Tahzay burst into view. Cochise looked fondly at his two sons. Nachise was a healthy youngster, and daily Tahzay grew sturdier. Within a few years Tahzay would begin the four raids as an apprentice, after which he would take his place among the warriors, and perhaps one day would follow his father as chief.

Tahzay already was expert with his boy's bow and arrow.

With the other children in the tribe, he worked endlessly to develop his body and make himself healthy and strong. When he reached manhood, Cochise thought, he would be able to accompany other warriors who could run miles without effort through the hard country.

"What do you do today?" Cochise asked Tahzay.

"There are contests."

"Win them."

"I will try, Father."

"I will be there to watch." As Tahzay flushed with pleasure, Cochise put his arm around him. "You must be strong, my son. You have only yourself to look to in this world. You may have many friends, but when the important time comes it is only your own legs and arms and ears and eyes that are friends. When you get in trouble do not look around and do not call upon anybody to help you. Look to yourself and if you have prepared yourself properly you need look no further."

Tahzay nodded, his young face very serious.

"Someday I hope you will be worthy to be the leader of your people," Cochise continued. "There will be many changes. Keep your eyes open and watch the changes and try to understand them. If you do not understand things, come and ask me. You will find enemies everywhere. You will thank enemies who are honest enough to say they are enemies. The worst enemies are those who say they are friends. Trust no man as friend until your eyes are clear enough to recognize friendship and your ears keen enough to know when a man speaks with a forked tongue. But when you have found a true friend, value him. He is worth more than your horse and your gun. A true friend comes but once, maybe, in a man's life. He is like a right arm. If he is lost he cannot be replaced. Remember all that and think about it.

"When you are a man it may be your people will be living in peace. I am working for this. But maybe it will not be that way. No matter how it is you must be prepared and you must be a leader and make everybody listen to you. Remember you are fit to lead your people only as long as you never forget that everything you do must be for their good." He pressed his son to him. "Now go to the race."

The contests were held in a small canyon. When Cochise arrived, there were eight boys standing in a line. Pionsenay was talking to them in his slow, drawling voice. In his hand he held a small gourd of water. He said: "Each of you take a mouthful. But do not swallow it. You are going to run four miles with this water in your mouth."

The eight boys, dwarfed by his bulk, nodded eagerly. They filled their mouths with water from the gourd, and then, at a signal from Pionsenay, they trotted off. Tahzay, his head erect, did not look at his father as he ran past him, graceful as a young deer. Pionsenay ran behind the boys to make sure they did not rest on the way. As he passed, Skinyea called out derisively: "Try to keep up with them, old cow!"

Pionsenay grunted. "Come along, little one, and I will carry you on my shoulder."

When the boys returned, they again lined up and as Pionsenay walked from one to the other, they spat the water on the ground. One boy had no water in his mouth. Pionsenay looked at him sternly. "What happened to you?"

"I stumbled and swallowed the water," the boy said miserably.

"Go to your wickiup," Pionsenay ordered.

The boy turned without a word. His father, sitting among the other men, rose and followed him in shame.

Now Pionsenay gave slings to the boys. "All right," he said. "This is going to make you quick. Divide into two bands."

The boys split up and got about seventy-five feet apart. Then, at a signal from Pionsenay, they picked up small stones, fitted them into the slings, and hurled them at each other. They had to throw the stones and dodge stones thrown at them at the same time. One of the stones struck a boy in the eye. Blood streamed down his face. The boy did not stop. With one eye blinded, he continued to dodge and hurl stones. Another stone struck a boy on the wrist. He tried to go on, but the pain was so great he dropped out.

After the sling practice the boys shot short arrows at each other. Then there was a foot race, to a point about four hundred yards and back. Tahzay won the foot race. He and the boy who came in second were given a privilege. They picked up two sticks. The race was held again and this time Tahzay and the other boy ran behind the contestants and whipped the slow boys across the ankles.

A warrior glanced at Cochise. He moved his finger idly on the ground. "I have a fine son," he said casually. "He is hard to beat."

"I have a good boy," Cochise said indifferently.

"I have a paint horse."

"My black one," Cochise said.

The challenge made and accepted, the warrior, named Machogee, called his son, and the boy and Tahzay faced each other. Other bets were made quickly among other men. The boys wrapped their wiry arms around each other and tried to force each other down. Machogee's son suddenly grasped Tahzay's wrist and twisted his arm around his back. He began to push Tahzay's arm upward. Tahzay bit his lips. The other boy pushed the arm farther and Tahzay's face twisted with pain as he struggled to keep from crying quits.

The warriors watched stolidly, offering no suggestions. The boy kept pushing until Tahzay felt his arm must break. Then Tahzay managed to twist around. He caught the other boy under the leg with his free arm and threw him down, causing him to release his grip. Before he could recover, Tahzay was on top of him, his knee digging into him, his arms pinning the other boy's shoulders to the earth.

Then Tahzay moved swiftly. He got a headlock on the other boy. He wrapped his legs around the other boy's waist and began to tighten them. The boy's face turned red and his eyes bulged.

The watching men made no sound.

Tahzay tightened his legs more. The other boy became limp, but he did not cry "Enough!" Tahzay squeezed still harder. The boy fainted. His head rolled to one side. Tahzay got up and Pionsenay threw some water on the other boy.

"It was brave," Cochise said. "He did not give up."

"I will bring the horse to you," Machogee said.

"No — he did not give up," Cochise said. "The bets are canceled."

Eight times Holos, the Sun, rose and set before Nahilzay returned to the rancheria with Gokliya and his warriors. Most of the men with Gokliya were strangers to the Chiricahuas. They were renegades from their own tribes.

Gokliya entered the camp of Cochise with a great show of boldness. He rode a beautiful gray horse and bore a Mexican military carbine. He dismounted and walked haughtily to Cochise. Other warriors gathered.

"This man walks well armed," Cochise said dryly.

"This country is said to be unkind to strangers," Gokliya retorted.

"There is no need for you to be stranger here. You grew to manhood here. Every rock knows you, even with the new name of Geronimo."

Gokliya looked around, pretending he could recognize nothing. "This place is strange to me. I know neither the rocks nor the people living here."

[44]

"Eyes may become clouded," Cochise said.

"My eyes are clear," Gokliya said angrily. "A cloud has descended and now covers the eyes of some people."

"I have given you safety," Cochise said softly. "Speak freely."

"Safety!" Gokliya sneered.

"There does not live on this earth any man who has ever questioned my word," Cochise said in the same soft voice. He let his eyes fall full upon the face of Gokliya and although the eyes of the Chiricahua chief were calm and mild Gokliya soon looked down.

"There was no intent to doubt your word," Gokliya said, hating himself for speaking so before his followers.

"I have heard that there are certain words you have used against me," Cochise said. "I do not like those words."

"Man speaks many words," Gokliya said.

"You know of the words I mean," Cochise said, still not raising his voice. "While you have cut yourself off from your own people and demand that you be called by the Mexican name Geronimo, you have not forgotten the ways of the Apaches. Among us there is no joking about things not of this earth."

Gokliya looked nervously at the Chiricahua warriors who now were listening intently. He moved slightly until he was closer to his own men.

Cochise's chest filled. "Do you have within you any of those words to repeat now?"

"I am in your camp, among your warriors," Gokliya said.

[45]

"My warriors will keep silent. I speak as one man to another man. Do you have any of those words left?"

Gokliya clenched his fists. "No."

"Then listen," Cochise said. "You grew up among us. Then you walked away. This is my country. Keep out of this country. You wear war paint on your face. Do you want to war with me?"

"No."

"Then we are not enemies. If you want to change your ways you may come back among us. But until then you will stay away. From this moment on if you or your men appear in my country, you will be killed at sight."

"It is well!" Gokliya said, fighting his rage.

"Go now in peace," Cochise said. "Do as you will elsewhere. Except for one thing: you never again will use the words you have used against me. It is understood?"

"Yes."

"Do not believe that words can be spoken and forgotten. If you say them again they will come back to me. And the day that they come I will swear an oath for your death — no matter where you hide yourself."

"They will not be spoken," Gokliya said.

"Go then and take your followers."

Gokliya hesitated. The words had been like lashes. He felt he had to say something to save his face before his men.

"Is there anything else you want to say?" Cochise asked politely.

Gokliya remained silent.

"Is there any challenge you want to make to me?" Cochise asked.

Gokliya remained silent. Then suddenly he raised his head and gave an agonized scream. He held his clenched fists at his sides and tears of fury fell upon his cheeks. Then he ran quickly to his horse and leaped upon it and hysterically kicked its sides and galloped out of the camp.

The men who had come with him watched this, and then half of them climbed silently on their own horses and departed. The others came to Cochise. One of them said: "We walk with you."

CHAPTER V

Two men, wearing sober black Eastern clothes, both showing signs of hard traveling, entered a saloon in Mesilla, in
New Mexico Territory. They looked around for a moment
and then walked up to a tall, spare, red-bearded man who
was leaning against the bar.

One of the new arrivals said: "I beg your pardon, sir.
But are you Captain Thomas Jeffords?"

The red-bearded man nodded slowly.

"Good!" the newcomer said heartily. He held out his
hand. "My name is William Buckley." Jeffords accepted
the handshake and Buckley continued: "This is Mr. Silas
St. John. We are both out here to represent the Butterfield
Stage Line."

[48]

"Glad to meet you," Jeffords murmured. He said to the bartender: "Set them up for the gentlemen, Pete."

Buckley took off his hat and wiped his forehead with his kerchief. "I'm glad we located you, Captain Jeffords." He picked up the drink the bartender set before him and drank it gratefully. He wiped his lips. Jeffords contemplated him quietly. Buckley said: "We're putting a line through to California — mail and passengers. St. John and I are prospecting the country, setting the route and establishing places for the depots."

"I heard about the Butterfield business," Jeffords said. "Pretty ambitious — going through Indian country."

St. John, a slender man with a thin, sensitive face, said: "We have been hoping that perhaps we could persuade you to help us, Captain Jeffords."

Jeffords looked surprised. "Me? I don't know anything about stage lines."

"From what we have learned about you we believe you could be of the greatest assistance to us, Captain Jeffords," St. John said. "We've heard a great deal about you — about your having been a riverboat captain — on the Great Lakes and on the Mississippi — how you have prospected in Indian country. We have been assured that you know the country here as few white men do."

"I've been around," Jeffords admitted.

"Then perhaps you'd be good enough to listen to our proposition," Buckley said.

"Let's sit down," Jeffords said.

When the three men were seated at a small table in a

far corner of the saloon, Buckley, a heavy-set man with dark eyes under black brows, said: "John Butterfield has a contract with the government to build this line and operate it. St. John here used to be connected with the old San Antonio and San Diego Line and when Butterfield took that over Silas agreed to come on in with us. We intend to run stages from St. Louis and Memphis all the way to San Francisco. We're almost complete up to this point and now we're planning to push through the Chiricahua and Dragoon Mountains to Tucson."

"Apache country," Jeffords said.

"Yes, Apache country," St. John said. "That's why we've been looking for you. We've been told that you not only know the country but that you know the Indians and understand them. They say you even speak some of the Indian dialect. You would be invaluable to us, Captain Jeffords."

"I'm not a stage-line man," Jeffords said. "I'm a prospector."

"There's good money in it," Buckley said.

Jeffords shook his head. "I don't think so."

Buckley's face fell. "May I ask why not?"

"I like it here," Jeffords said.

"Like Mesilla? What is there to like in Mesilla? Nothing but Mexicans. Before the year is out Tucson will be a bigger town than this."

"I like it here," Jeffords repeated pleasantly.

"We'll make it worth your while," Buckley pressed.

"Thanks, gentlemen, but no. There's a new place I found up one of these mountains. I want to poke around a little."

St. John leaned forward. "Is there any offer we can make to you? We know nothing about the Apaches."

"I'll think about it," Jeffords said.

"Will you, sir? The main depot for this section of the line will be in Tucson. If you change your mind will you come over and see us there?"

Buckley stood up, his face showing his disappointment.

"I'm sorry you feel as you do, Captain Jeffords," he said. "But I'll be traveling back and forth between here and Tucson for some little time to come. We sure could use you." He looked down at St. John. "Coming?"

"I'd like to talk to Captain Jeffords for a little longer if he is not too busy," St. John said.

"Not at all," Jeffords said.

After Buckley left, St. John said: "I don't want to take up any of your time, Captain Jeffords. But your interest in the Indians fascinates me."

Jeffords looked at St. John keenly. "Most white men don't try to find out anything about Indians. It's not a very popular subject in this part of the country."

"It's curious," St. John said. "Men out here talk about Indians the way they speak of Negroes in the South."

"Just about."

"I've tried to learn something about Indians. I've tried to find out what makes white men hate them so much. From what I've been able to see the average white man out here refuses to admit the Indian is a human being."

Jeffords studied St. John for a few moments. "If we ever tried to understand what makes Indians think as they do, we'd all get along better. And maybe a few more people on both sides would stay alive."

Early in August, 1858, Buckley, St. John and a party of American and Mexican workers set out with an eight-wagon mule train from Mesilla and headed westward. It was in the full summer heat. The mule train crossed the Rio Grande and at a place called Cooks Spring, about fifty miles on the way, several of the men and one of the wagons were left to construct a station. The train continued and twenty miles farther crossed the Mimbres River. Seventeen miles beyond that at Cow Springs another wagon and group of men remained to build a depot there. Thirty-odd miles beyond, at Soldier's Farewell Springs, still another group was left off.

From Soldier's Farewell the wagons rolled across the metal-hard country up to Stein's Peak, near what later became the boundary between New Mexico and Arizona, and there, in a little hollow, Buckley ordered that another depot be built. Since this area was known to be the favorite hunting ground of Mangas Coloradas, he ordered that a substantial station be built, with a stone corral and fortified buildings.

Throughout the journey, Buckley was tense and nervous. Shadows, stones, rocks in the distance, all made him start and reach for his rifle. St. John tried to lighten his mood lest it spread to the other men. Buckley scarcely listened to him.

As they made their camp at Stein's Peak, Buckley said: "So far, so good."

"Indians seldom attack a party as strong as ours," St. John said reassuringly. "We're almost a small troop. And we ought to hit Apache Pass before long. We'll be in Chiricahua country then."

"Cochise," Buckley said.

"Cochise is at peace."

"I'll believe an Apache is peaceful when I see him dead," Buckley said.

In the morning the men started for Apache Pass. Buckley and St. John, who had stood guard during the early morning hours, went to sleep in one of the wagons. Two hours out of Stein's Peak, they were wakened by a violent jolt.

"Axle's broken," Buckley said. He jumped out of the wagon, followed by St. John. He saw that they were alone. "Where are the other wagons?" he demanded of the driver.

"Over the hill. They got a little ahead of us."

"Over the hill! I told you to keep close to the wagon in front of you."

"I been having trouble with the mules," the driver said.

"How far ahead do you figure they are?"

"Not too far."

"Run up that hill and fire your rifle. I want them back here!" Buckley bent down to look at the broken axle and as he did so he heard a whine and an arrow splintered the wooden frame of the wagon just above his head. He looked back and saw that they were surrounded by Indians.

"Get inside the wagon, everyone!" St. John ordered. "Get inside and keep your heads down!"

The men clambered into the wagon. "Apaches?" Buckley asked.

"I think so," St. John said coolly. "We're not finished yet. There are five of us and five men with rifles can hold off this gang for quite a while. The noise of the shooting ought to bring back the others."

"They're too far away by now," Buckley groaned.

The Indians now were circling the wagon, leaning over the far side of their ponies and firing under the ponies' necks. One of the men in the wagon cried out. He tore at his throat. An arrow had pierced his neck, the point coming out under his ear. He stopped clawing and died.

"That leaves four!" Buckley said. Then he shouted: "My God, look!" He pointed to the crest of the hill. "More of them!"

St. John peered over the wagon. "They're shooting at the other Indians! Hold your fire, men! Our friends have stopped bothering us and they're trying to fight off the newcomers!"

Lying in the wagon, the Americans watched as the second band of Indians closed in on the men who had attacked the wagon. There was a quick exchange of bullets and arrows and then the first band broke ground and raced away.

"What do we do now?" Buckley asked.

"Wait and see," St. John said. "Look at that big Indian

in the front. He's holding out his hand. That's the peace sign."

"It's a trick," Buckley said. "They just want to get us out of the wagon." He raised his rifle. "They're not fooling me."

St. John pushed down the gun quickly. "Keep that down!" He climbed out of the wagon. He laid his own rifle plainly against the wagon and walked toward the tall Indian, holding out his hands.

The Indian jumped from his horse. "Cochise," he said.

St. John's eyes widened. He pointed to the Indian. "Cochise?"

The Indian shook his head. He gestured to the west.

"Bill," St. John called.

Buckley lifted his head slightly. "Yes?"

"This Indian is trying to tell me he wants to take us to Cochise," St. John said.

"It's a trick!"

"Maybe not," St. John said. "But we don't have any choice. If we try to fight it will end up only one way. I think we'll have to go along with them."

The men got out of the wagon, looking with suspicion at the Indians, and set to work to replace the broken axle shaft. The big Indian watched them and then grunted something to his men. Several of the Indians went to the wagon and raised the rear end and held it while the new axle was put in place.

The dead American was buried and Buckley said gloomily, "Well, let's go. Only God knows where we'll end up!"

Guided by the Indians, they rode for several hours. They entered a pass. It was late afternoon, and the sun had passed to the far side of the long cut. Presently the Indians turned into another canyon that cut off to one side of the pass. They rode for another hour. The quick twilight ended and it was dark. The wagon jolted over rough country, through gullies and up and down hills. And then suddenly they were in an Indian camp. Buckley looked around with dismay. "Indians," he said. "Hundreds of them."

The wagon was led to the center of the camp. Indians clustered around and looked at it curiously. Then a tall, lean man approached. The big Indian began to speak to him rapidly. The tall man nodded and his face tightened with anger. Then he walked up to the Americans and said something to them. He looked from face to face. The Americans shook their heads. The Indian said something in Spanish.

St. John said instantly, "I have some Spanish." The tall Indian spoke for several minutes. When he finished, St. John said: "He says that he is Cochise. He says that these are his people. The Chiricahua people are at peace with the Americans, he says, and tomorrow he will take us to some white soldiers. He says that he saw our other wagons going through the pass earlier. He says he is sorry for what happened to us, and that we were attacked by renegade Apaches led by a man named Geronimo, and that he is happy his own warriors came along in time to save our lives."

"Tell him to bring us to the troops tonight," Buckley

said instantly. "I don't want to spend the night in an Apache camp."

"I think not," St. John said. "We have to accept his hospitality the way he is offering it."

"I'm running this job!" Buckley said angrily. "Tell him we want to get out of here tonight!"

"These men have had it in their power to kill us at any time," St. John said. "This man does not mean trouble. Unless we force it on him. I'm afraid you'll have to trust my judgment in this, Bill."

As they spoke, Cochise watched them sharply, his eyes moving to each man as he spoke. There was a faint trace of a smile on his face as he cut in and spoke to St. John. When he finished, St. John said: "He understands what we're arguing about. He says we'll be safe here."

Buckley exhaled heavily. "All right."

St. John walked to the wagon and put his rifle inside. The other men followed his example. Then Cochise pointed to the campfire. "Eat," he said.

St. John nodded and walked with the Indian leader to the fire. St. John found that for some reason he trusted Cochise — and what surprised him more, he discovered that he was enjoying this new experience. He looked around with great interest, smiling at the women and patting the heads of the children who came up to him. One lad in particular caught his eyes. Cochise said: "This is my son, Tahzay."

St. John nodded. "I see in his face the younger face of his father."

Women brought roast meat and corn cakes. The white men ate their fill and when Buckley finished he wiped his lips and lighted a cigar. "That wasn't too bad," he said. "At least I'll die with a full stomach."

"What do you think it was?" St. John asked.

"Some kind of game, I guess. Venison, maybe."

"It was mule meat," St. John said.

Buckley got up suddenly and walked away, holding his mouth.

After the others turned in Cochise and St. John spoke with each other for a long time, using their imperfect Spanish, and Tahzay crouched at their feet and tried to understand what was being said.

When the Americans woke in the morning they found the camp was already astir. Buckley drank coffee and ate biscuits but would touch nothing else. Cochise and ten or twelve warriors rode up and said they were ready to lead the wagon to the soldiers. They set out and rode for most of the morning. The sun was high when Cochise raised his long arm. The wagon rolled up a hill and then on a nearby slope they saw the camp of an American military patrol. Cochise galloped forth alone. When he came to the camp he dismounted and stood silently by his horse. A moment later Major Steen was at his side. The two men embraced.

"I have a wagon and four of your countrymen," Cochise said. "They were attacked by a bad Apache named Gokliya, who now calls himself Geronimo."

"How did you know where to find us?"

Cochise smiled. "The birds told me."

"I wish the birds would speak to me," Steen said. "It appears that you can put your hand on us anytime, no matter where we are in this country of yours."

"There are many birds," Cochise said.

Steen sent a soldier up the hill to bring the other men down. In a few minutes the wagon rumbled into the camp and Buckley jumped out and seized Steen's hand, shaking it violently.

"You don't know how glad I am to see you, Major," Buckley said fervently.

"Enoch Steen, First Dragoons, at your service, sir."

"I'm Bill Buckley. Out here for the Butterfield people. We've had quite an experience, Major, but it's over now!"

"Thanks to Cochise," Steen said.

"The white man has not been happy in our company," Cochise said.

"I think you owe your life to this man, Mr. Buckley," Steen said quietly. "He has pledged himself to protect the stage route through Chiricahua country and I think he has shown he means to keep his word. If you represent the Butterfield people you will be making the greatest mistake of your life if you do not win the friendship of this man. Believe me, sir, the success or failure of your venture lies with this Indian leader." Steen turned to Cochise and put his arm on his shoulder. "I have been looking for you," he said. "I have received orders to leave Fort Buchanan."

"The news is bad," Cochise said. "Where do you go?"

"Many days' journey from here. I have been ordered to go to a school for more learning."

Cochise waved his arm. "This is your school."

"I believe so too. But I must obey orders."

"Who will be the new *nantan* at the fort?"

"I do not know. But he will be a friend to Cochise."

"I have a warning that it will not be as good."

"From another of your birds?"

"A bird of bad luck."

"You must not believe that," Steen said earnestly. "Whoever is the new commandant — he will want to continue the peace."

"Maybe," Cochise said.

"I know it to be so." Steen smiled. "I have something for you. A farewell present." He took a leather tube from his saddlebag and uncapped one end. He extracted a rolled-up paper.

"The picture writing," Cochise said.

"You will remember me by it," Steen said.

"I wait for the day when you will return," Cochise said.

"I wait for that day. You have been a good friend, Cochise. You are a man of truth and honor." He said to Buckley: "Are your people aiming to build a station here?"

"We want to put one up in Apache Pass and another at Dragoon Springs," Buckley said.

"Do you want to speak to Cochise about it?"

"Why would I want to speak to an Apache about a stage line?"

St. John said: "You are quite right, Major. Let me speak to Cochise."

Steen turned his back on Buckley. "You may use my interpreter, sir," he said to St. John.

"We get along quite well in Spanish," St. John said. He faced Cochise. "We want to pass through the Chiricahua country. It is our hope that the chief of the Chiricahua Apaches will not object to our building stations at Apache Pass and Dragoon Springs."

"I have given my word," Cochise said, his eyes on Buckley. "My warriors will cause no trouble."

"It is our hope that when the station is completed in Apache Pass that the Chiricahua people will come there often and be friends with the Americans," St. John said. "There will be a trading store there — many things that Apaches like. When the store is opened we will be honored if the Chiricahua people will come to us and receive gifts."

"I will tell my people," Cochise said.

"I do not thank the Chiricahua chief for saving our lives," St. John said. "Some things are greater than any thanks. I hope that the Chiricahua chief always is protected from danger, but if he should find himself in danger I hope that I may in some way do for him what he has done for us."

"We are friends," Cochise said.

St. John went to the wagon and took a new Wesson carbine from it. He gave it to Cochise.

"This is a good thing," Cochise said. He looked at Steen and at Buckley and then at Steen again. "This is a good thing," he repeated. He embraced Steen again and shook St. John's hand. He leaped lightly upon his horse and he held the carbine in the air. *"Hasta luego, amigos,"* he said. He rode up to Steen. *"Adiós."*

"*Adiós,* Cochise," Steen said.

The Indians rode swiftly up the hillside.

CHAPTER VI

Cochise walked slowly toward his wickiup. Ghost Face was heavy and cold on the land. He paused in front of the skin dwelling and watched Tahzay try to teach Nachise how to use a bow and arrow. He entered the wickiup. He said to Tesalbestinay: "I have been asked to bring all the people down to the trading post in Apache Pass. The Americans want to give them presents."

"It will make the people happy," Tesalbestinay said. "They need happiness."

The new stage line had been operating for about three months through the Chiricahua country. On four different occasions Cochise's warriors had come to the rescue of

American travelers who were attacked by enemy Indians. Now, as St. John had promised, the Americans desired to show their gratitude for the friendship of Cochise.

The word of the invitation passed from family to family. It was received with joy. The Indians were still finding it hard to follow the new path their leader had drawn for them. There were more Americans than ever before and wild game was growing scarcer all the time. Ranchers appropriated water holes for their cattle so that the wild animals could find no place to drink. The Apaches had never planted corn and there was hunger among them.

Hoping that the invitation would give his people something to take their minds off their troubles, Cochise led his people to the new station in Apache Pass on a clear day in December. The Indians were dressed in their best. Their deerskin blouses were freshly dyed. They wore new thigh-high moccasins, folded at the knees to make a kind of circular pocket. Their ponies were curried and on the slender legs of the animals were newly-made deerskin boots.

The Butterfield Station in Apache Pass had been constructed with several rooms. One room served as living quarters for the Butterfield agent, Hank Culver, a big, red-faced, good-natured man, and for his hostler, Fred Walsh, a stocky Californian. The second room was used as a storeroom and contained feed for the mules which were kept in the corral as replacements for the tired animals which brought in the coaches. The third room was a public lounge for travelers.

Cochise rode at the head of his people. His black eyes

were bright and his face was peaceful and happy. This meeting symbolized to him the friendship he had established with the Americans. At his side was Tahzay, and with Tesalbestinay was Nachise. Behind them rode Nahilzay, Juan, Pionsenay, Skinyea and Naretena, and other warriors, and behind them walked the women and children, laughing with excitement.

Hank Culver walked out of the corral gate and met Cochise about a hundred yards from the station. He welcomed the Apaches and led them inside the station walls, where the warriors seated themselves in a circle. Cochise was given the place of honor on folded blankets. To his right were his warriors in the order of their importance. To his left were the Americans.

"This is a happy day," Culver said. "Nowhere is there a greater chief than Cochise. And nowhere are there greater warriors than the Chiricahuas. It might have been that the Chiricahuas and the Americans would continue as enemies. Instead, through the wisdom of the great Cochise, we sit together as brothers, in peace with each other, and the women and children of the tribe walk among us without fear. And when Americans travel in the country of Cochise they are secure because they know the wise and powerful Cochise is their friend and protector."

A "tame" Apache boy named Tali translated the speech, which had been prepared for Culver by St. John in Tucson.

When Culver finished, Cochise replied that his people would continue to befriend and guard over Americans. There were more speeches and then the Americans brought out presents: bundles of red flannel cloth, blankets, calico, sacks of corn, barley and dried beef. For the children there were trinkets and sweets.

By February the tribe was without food. Hunters roamed everywhere over the snow-covered hills, but there was no sign. A rabbit might be shot — a squirrel picked off in the lowlands — but the big game was not there.

Cochise sent men to the West Stronghold to get some of the dried meat that was cached there for emergency. This food lasted through the worst days of the winter, and when the cold weather broke at last and Little Eagles looked in on the land and then decided to remain, Cochise called for a large-scale raid in Mexico to cheer his dispirited people.

The announcement brought the greatest joy. The men shook off their discontent and set to work to ready their weapons and other equipment. In the household of Cochise there was another kind of excitement. This would be the first raid on which Tahzay would accompany the warriors as a novice.

The tall, thoughtful boy tried to cover his joy with a suitable show of manly indifference. He made arrows — although as a novice he would not participate directly in the raid except in an emergency. His duties would be to serve the warriors as they needed him. The fact that he was the son of the chief made no difference, except that he would have to work harder than another boy might. While he served as a novice any warrior had the right to give him an order and he would be expected to obey.

Cochise and his brother Naretena watched the boy work at his arrows. Tesalbestinay looked knowingly at Cochise, and then asked with a great show of innocence: "Is this a journey for children?"

Tahzay flushed. He kept his eyes on his work.

"We are only going to make a friendly call," Cochise said.

"I wondered why you were taking a small boy with you," Tesalbestinay said.

"Perhaps you would like to come, wife," Cochise said. "There will be no danger."

"No," she said. "I will stay here and defend the camp, maybe. It might be more dangerous here."

Sweat started to creep on the neck of Tahzay but he said nothing. Then Naretena said: "Pay no attention, Tahzay. They are proud of you."

Cochise laughed with pretended scorn. "Proud? At his age, when I was a young man, one had a wife and was full warrior."

"Young people do not develop so quickly these days," Tesalbestinay said. "It is a wonder that girls look at them."

The chaffing was the traditional prelude for a boy going out on his first raid. Tahzay would have been disappointed if his father and mother had omitted it, but it still was embarrassing.

"I hear that the father of Oraya expects one of the warriors to ask for her hand in marriage soon," Tesalbestinay said.

Tahzay thought he would sink into the earth. Oraya was a pretty girl to whom he had completely lost his heart.

"One of the leaders will want her, maybe," Cochise agreed. "Nahilzay or Pionsenay. They are rich men and they can afford a wife."

Then Cochise called his son to him and held him to him and the laughter departed from his face. When Cochise spoke his voice was serious. "You are a good son." he said. "I am proud of you. Our people are proud of you. They say good things about you. They say you will be a good leader later on, maybe. You have a strong body, and most important you have a heart that belongs inside a man and I am proud of you."

The boy's eyes were shining. He bit his lips to keep from showing his emotion.

Cochise said: "It is necessary sometimes for a man to tell his son many things when he goes on his first raid. I have to tell you very little. You have learned your lessons well. There is nothing I have to say. I have no fear for your conduct."

Tahzay returned to his work without allowing himself to thank his father or tell him how his words stirred his blood. He glanced around the wickiup, filled with the evidences of his father's greatness in the field: saddles, bridles, quirts, saddlebags, bows, arrows, quivers, shields, wrist-guards, spears, slings, knives. Standing in a corner were two of Cochise's prize possessions: his double-barreled shotgun and the carbine Silas St. John had given to him.

Cochise gestured to Tesalbestinay and she left the wickiup. Presently she returned and handed a deerskin-covered bundle to Cochise. He said: "My son."

Tahzay stood up. "Yes, Father."

"You work well on arrows," Cochise said. "What I have here is not needed, maybe." He opened the bundle and took from it a long bow, almost full size. For weeks Cochise had worked on it secretly, cutting it from an oak branch in a distant part of the camp. He had split the branch, had shaped and smoothed the wood, and after it was dried, had greased and limbered it. Then he had curved it and had tied it with a thong and had placed it on hot ashes, watching carefully so that it would not burn. After that he had buried it for ten days to get its shape fully into it.

When the bow was ready for decoration, Cochise had boiled animal hoofs and horns and from the glue he had sealed to the shaft pieces of sinew, in the middle and near the ends. Then he had painted the outside a bright red and on the inside he had drawn stars and crosses. Finally he tied the sinew from the loin of a deer to both ends of the bow.

Now Tahzay took the bow. His jaw muscles worked. His father then handed him four arrows made of mulberry. Eagle feathers were attached to the arrows. Cochise said: "It is not intended that you shoot any arrows in the raid. If it is necessary to do so, however, you will use these arrows before all others."

Tahzay knew this was the most solemn moment of his life. No matter what happened to him in the time to come, nothing would be as important. His father gave him a wrist-guard made of buckskin, an arrow quiver, and a spear made of spruce. The final gift was a fine steel knife in a buckskin sheath, obtained by Cochise from the trading post in Apache Pass.

"I will use all of these in a manner that will bring no shame to you," Tahzay said. Then, because he could no longer control his emotions, he asked for permission to leave the wickiup, and he hurried out.

From the moment the adobe walls of the hacienda in Mexico were sighted, Tahzay felt a calm come over him. It was possible, he thought, that his death might lie before those guarded walls, but it did not matter. The only thing that mattered was that he was at last riding at the side of his father, Cochise, and that he was the son of Cochise, and that if he had to start the dark journey at this time it would be under the eyes of Cochise. He could know no fear.

The attack was made, as usual, at dawn. The Indians circled the walls of the hacienda, concentrating on the corral where fat mules looked out calmly at the galloping men. When the fighting began, Tahzay became the servant of the warriors. He carried messages from Cochise to his lieutenants. He brought water to thirsty and wounded men. He worked coolly and calmly and the eyes of his father looked upon him with approval.

In one of his trips from Cochise to Nahilzay, who was leading one band of the Indians, Tahzay was trapped by four Mexicans. The son of Cochise then worked swiftly with his arrows, using first the four his father had given to him. The Mexicans retreated under the cold deadliness of his attack and the Indians who had witnessed what had happened thought that Tahzay might have been Cochise himself, when he was a youth.

On the return, leading captured mules, the Indians were attacked by Mexican soldiery. The Mexicans were beaten off but half a dozen Indians were killed. The incident plunged Cochise into gloom. Although the warriors were loaded with plunder, the raid now had become a costly one.

His face was heavy as he turned to his son and spoke to him, as one man to another. "You did well today, my son," Cochise said.

Tahzay waved his hand toward the captured booty. "We all did well, I think."

Cochise rode in silence for a few moments and then he said: "I would give it all back if I could bring back the lives of the men who were killed. And yet they died as men and that is something."

Cochise was lost in his thoughts as the warriors made their way back to the camp. Perhaps in some way he could arrange for his warriors to do some work for the Americans. If that could be arranged, there would be less and less need to raid in Mexico. Men who might have been killed would live, and the Chiricahua tribe, smallest of all the Apache tribes, would increase in numbers instead of growing smaller each year.

It would be difficult to do, he knew — to persuade Apache fighting men to work for Americans. And yet it might be done.

The dancing and the singing had begun by the time the warriors reached camp. Cochise dismounted and handed his horse and weapons to Tesalbestinay. Then Tahzay climbed down from his pony and started to lead it to the corral. His mother stopped him. "You have begun life as a warrior," she said. She took his weapons from him and then the reins of his pony. She led both animals away.

Then, his head very high, the son of Cochise stood by the side of his father and listened to the singing of the people.

CHAPTER VII

Hank Culver, the Butterfield agent at Apache Pass, looked at the cloud of dust in the distance. "Wonder who that can be," he said.

Walsh, the hostler, who was feeding mules in the corral, squinted in the direction Culver was pointing. Then he said: "Looks like soldiers to me."

"Why soldiers?" Culver asked. "Things are quiet."

One of the stage drivers, a man named Clay Wallace, who often stopped off at the Apache Pass station, bit off the end of a cigar and lit it. "First time I ever saw a mounted patrol around here," he said.

"No need for soldiers if there is no trouble," Culver said. "And there's been no trouble with Cochise around."

Walsh said: "They got a civilian with them. Looks to me like it's Johnny Ward, from Sonoita."

"They tell me that Ward is a bad actor," Wallace said.

The three men waited until the soldiers drew up. The second lieutenant in command of the troop touched the brim of his hat. "I am George Bascom, Seventh Infantry. I would like some water for my men and horses."

Culver waved his hand in a friendly gesture. "Sure, Lieutenant, help yourself. I'm Hank Culver, Station Agent here."

Bascom dismounted. He gave orders to his first sergeant, a burly man named Reuben Bernard, to take the men and animals to the spring. Then Bascom said to Culver: "I am going to make camp not far from here. I would like to meet the Indian, Cochise."

Culver looked puzzled. "Cochise? Why do you want to see him?"

Bascom ignored the question. "He hangs around here, does he not, Mr. Culver?"

"He has a camp in the mountains," Culver said. "His men have been working for us, supplying us with firewood."

"Does he come down here often?"

"Once in a while. They cut wood for us and bring it down and trade it for stuff they need."

"Well, when you see him again, tell him the white flag is flying over my tent and that I want to speak to him," Bascom said coldly.

He mounted and rode off. It was a bright, cloudless day in the early part of February, 1861.

About an hour after the troop rode off, Cochise came

down to the station. With him were Naretena, Tesalbestinay, Tahzay, and two grown sons of Juan. It was a hot day and the men wore nothing but breechclouts. Cochise greeted Culver and sat down in the shade. After a few minutes Cochise said: "Soldiers were here."

Wallace, who had become friendly with Cochise and who had picked up a good deal of Apache language, said: "From Fort Buchanan. The officer in command said he was going to make camp near here and that he would like you to visit with him."

Cochise raised his head quickly, like a hunting dog on a strange scent.

"He said to tell you the white flag was flying over his tent," Wallace said.

Cochise relaxed. He said to Naretena: "The new chief at Buchanan who was sent to take the place of Nantan Steen must have sent these soldiers. They must have come to tell us the new *nantan* wants to be a friend."

Naretena nodded. "That is it."

"We will go and visit with the new soldier *nantan*," Cochise said. "Do you have enough wood?"

"We could use more," Culver said. "The nights get cold."

"Good. We will visit with the new soldier and then we will return to our camp and cut more wood for you."

"Do you need anything from the store?" Culver asked. "New red flannel has just arrived."

"When we bring down the firewood we will take some," Cochise said.

Lieutenant Bascom stood in front of the tent he had had erected. A white flag, traditional and sacred sign of peace, fluttered over the tent. Johnny Ward, the rancher from Sonoita, a big redheaded man, pointed. "There comes Cochise," he said.

Bascom looked down the trail. He saw four men, a youth, and a woman. "Which one is Cochise?"

"The one in front," Ward said.

"That is Cochise?"

"Yeah. Surprised?"

Bascom shook his head. He was a young fresh-faced youth, only a short time out of West Point. He was ashamed to tell Ward that he had expected an Indian chief to look like an Indian chief. The people walking toward him looked like tramps. "So that's the great Cochise," he said in disgust.

The Indians walked into the army camp without fear. The white flag was flying plainly and it had been so long since Cochise had trouble with white men that he was without suspicion. He was certain this was the routine ceremonial visit. He expected the usual presents and expressions of friendship.

He walked into the tent, followed by the other Indians. Bascom and Ward, and an Indian interpreter named Antonio, were inside the tent. The Indians took places on the ground and sat silently.

When the Indians were inside, Bascom nodded to Ward and the rancher left the tent. Outside he motioned to Sergeant Bernard. "The lieutenant says to surround the tent with soldiers, Sergeant."

Bernard frowned. "Why does he want that? He has Cochise in there under a white flag."

"I don't know, Sergeant," Ward said nastily. "But you better obey orders."

Shaking his head, Bascom stationed twelve soldiers around the tent. When Ward saw that the order had been carried out he went back into the tent and nodded to Bascom. Then without further wait, Bascom spoke out. "Cochise, your Indians raided the ranch of this man, John Ward. You stole his child, named Mickey Free, and some oxen and horses. I have come here to get them all back."

When the words were translated Cochise stiffened and his eyes blazed. Then, looking at the childish face of the lieutenant, he controlled himself. He sat silent for a while, thinking on the words Bascom had used. Tesalbestinay put out her hand to quiet him. At last Cochise drew a deep breath. When he spoke his voice was unangry, but the friendliness was gone from his face.

"For more than five harvests my people have been at peace with the white man," Cochise said. "During that time no one belonging to the Chiricahua people has taken any child or animal or anything else belonging to Americans. Tell me what the boy looked like and I will send messengers to other Indian tribes and try to find him for you."

"Mr. Ward says it was Chiricahua Indians who raided his place," Bascom retorted.

Cochise made himself more comfortable. He was in no hurry. The matter had to be settled. It would take time because he could see that the officer with the baby face was not reasonable and was not wise. "My people have not been at war with Americans for more than five harvests," he said again. He felt that perhaps when the officer realized how impossible the accusation was he would apologize and then together they could make plans to recover the child and livestock.

"No Chiricahua men took the child," Naretena said. "It is as he says. There has been no conflict between our peoples for a long time."

"I have helped the Americans often," Cochise said. "I will be glad to do so now. If the child is described to me, and the kind and number of animals, I will send men to the Pinal Apaches and to the Tontos and Mescaleros and Coyoteros and other tribes and if the child is with one of them I will have it returned."

Cochise's quiet sincerity began to make an impression on Bascom. The officer looked at Ward with indecision. Ward said viciously: "The cutthroat is lying!" Ward stopped Antonio from translating the words but Cochise caught their sound and his eyes narrowed. He looked at Tahzay.

Naretena spoke again and then one of Juan's sons spoke and then the other son. Tahzay looked at his father and Cochise inclined his head. Tahzay said: "I have not been away from our people in many days. No child of any American has been brought to our camp — nor animals."

Cochise spoke again. He felt a chill going through him.

[78]

The talk was not going well. His hawk eyes saw the disbelief in the eyes of the boy officer, disbelief that was encouraged by Ward. He felt a numbness in the air. His attitude was sensed by the others and Tahzay felt an icy shiver pass through him.

Bascom, listening to the dusty, sweaty men in front of him, felt more and more cocky. He began to grow tired of the tedious Indian manner of speaking. He felt he had allowed the filthy creatures talk enough. For more than an hour they had done nothing but deny all knowledge of the kidnaping of the child. He decided the time had come to make a decisive move. He said suddenly: "Cochise, you are a damned liar!"

The blood fled from the face of the Chiricahua chief. His heart began to pound violently. For a moment he thought he could not breathe.

Bascom misunderstood his silence. He snarled again: "You are a damned liar!" Then, after a glance through the open vent of the tent, to make certain the soldiers were on guard, he said: "You and your people will be my prisoners until the Ward child is returned!"

The words were not fully translated when Cochise leaped to his feet with a piercing scream of rage. "I am no prisoner of yours!" he shouted. He whipped out a long knife from his breechclout and with a powerful sweep of his arm slashed open the tent. He cried to the other Indians: "Follow me!" And before Bascom or Ward knew what he was doing he leaped through the opening and shouldered his way past the bewildered soldiers outside.

He crouched low, running zigzag, Indian fashion, and the soldiers, as soon as they collected themselves, fired their carbines. One of the balls struck him in the leg as he dodged and twisted among the trees and rocks. He continued to run, leaving a thin trail of blood, until he crossed over a hill.

Tahzay pushed his mother through the tent to follow his father, but by then the soldiers were ready for them. Naretena was knocked down by a gun butt and one of Juan's sons was stabbed in the belly with a bayonet. The Indians were all captured.

Sergeant Bernard, who was inspecting the horses in another part of the camp, hurried back to the tent. He rushed up to Bascom, and the lieutenant, who was confused and a little frightened at what he had started, shouted: "Sergeant, turn out the detachment. Cochise escaped. Go after him and bring him back!"

Bernard looked at the white flag, still waving over the tent. He held back the first words that came to his lips. "There will be trouble, Lieutenant. We better get down to the station and warn the men there."

"I ordered you to go after Cochise!" Bascom said in fury.

"He is gone now, sir," Bernard said. "We'll never get him now. Believe me, sir, it's better to get down to the stage depot and warn those men. There might be real trouble."

"All right," Bascom said. "Get going."

Once in the hills, Cochise collected some of his warriors. He was still crazy with rage but he made himself think carefully. He did not want war with the Americans. It was ridiculous to go to war with the Americans, to destroy all he had built over the last years, because a stupid child had disbelieved his word. When he thought of what the lieutenant had called him he trembled — but he made himself calm down. The first thing was to recover his wife and son and his two nephews and his brother. After that the matter could be settled with an older and wiser representative of the American army.

On horse, a score of men behind him, he trotted down to the stage depot. He thought if he could capture the three men there he could use them to exchange for the members of his party. Later he could explain to the stage men why he had done what he had done. They would understand.

He appeared at the crest of the hill above the Butterfield station. He called out: "Culver! Agent Culver!"

When the agent stepped out Cochise motioned for him to come to him. Knowing nothing yet of what Bascom had done, Culver, who was joined by Walsh, walked over to where the Indians waited. The Americans were in their shirt sleeves, and were unarmed.

As they reached the Indians, Cochise signaled, and the warriors seized them. The Americans fought back instinctively. They knocked over two of the Indians who had dismounted to capture them, and then fled back to the station. The Indians, in wild excitement, fired. A ball struck Culver as he reached the station. He fell through the open door.

At that moment, Sergeant Bernard arrived with the troops on the other side of the depot. The soldiers climbed over the wall of the corral and crept around the building. They heard the shots from the Indians. One of the soldiers pulled Culver into the building. Just then Walsh, who had run off in another direction, reached the wall of the corral. He climbed over it. As his head appeared, a trooper, mistaking it for the head of an Indian, fired. Walsh fell dead, hanging over the wall.

When Cochise saw that the depot now was occupied by soldiers, he pulled his men back out of gun range. He paused on the hilltop and looked down. He struggled to keep himself calm. He had seen Culver fall and had seen Walsh shot and he knew that things were passing from his control. He thought of his five people held by Bascom. He had to get Americans to trade for them.

The aimless horror of the last few hours welled up inside of him. He lifted his head and gave a wild Apache cry of fury and then he turned his horse and tore away.

CHAPTER VIII

C ochise followed a secret trail to the Stronghold. On the way he encountered Nahilzay with another small band of warriors. Cochise told Nahilzay what had happened. Then Cochise said: "Near Apache Pass there are nine wagons. Take your men and capture the Americans. Take them alive. I want no more Americans killed."

Nahilzay's eyes glittered. Not for many years had Chiricahuas fought in their own country. "I obey," he said.

"Remember, there are to be no Americans killed," Cochise repeated sternly. "This thing has gone far — but not too far. It can still be saved."

"I will kill no white-eyes," Nahilzay said, using the Apache's most hateful expression for Americans.

Nahilzay galloped away with his men. Pionsenay rode up soon after and told Cochise that the stagecoach from Tucson was on its way to the station in Apache Pass.

"There is a little wooden bridge over a ravine," Cochise said immediately. "Knock it down. Then when the stage is halted take the passengers prisoners. But no one must be killed!"

Pionsenay took ten or twelve men and hurried to the bridge, a narrow span crossing a steep chasm. The Indians knocked off the guard-rails and then hid themselves.

The coach appeared. The Indians opened fire at the mules. One of the lead mules was killed in the first volley. The stage driver was wounded in the leg. William Buckley, the line superintendent who had been rescued by Cochise's men three years earlier, when he and Silas St. John were attacked by Geronimo, was in the coach. He took the reins away from the wounded driver and pulled the coach to a halt. Passengers in the stage fought off the Indians while one man ran out and cut away the dead mule.

Then Buckley whipped the remaining mules and the coach lurched off. The Indians fired again, trying to cut down the other mules. The passengers returned the fire.

Buckley raced toward the bridge. The mules tore down the steep hill leading to the span. Buckley saw that the guard-rails were down. Behind him were Pionsenay and his men. Buckley whipped the mules again. They clattered across the bridge. The coach slipped off to one side, sliding on its axles, the right wheels dangling off the bridge.

Buckley whipped the animals again and again. Maddened, the mules pulled harder. They dragged the wagon across the bridge and then the wagon wheels bit into the hard, far side of the ravine and again regained the roadway. Pionsenay and his men pulled up at the edge of the chasm and screamed their disappointment.

Never slacking his whipping, Buckley drove the coach to the Apache Pass station. In front of the corral one of the mules fell dead of exhaustion. The wounded driver was carried into the station. The passengers took shelter. Buckley looked around. He yelled to Clay Wallace, the driver: "What in the name of God is going on around here?"

"Cochise," Wallace said. "Trouble."

"Cochise! I knew this would happen! The treacherous murderer!" Buckley raised his clenched fists. "I said from the beginning that he couldn't be trusted!"

The Indian prisoners captured by Lieutenant Bascom were thrown into the storeroom at the station. The son of Juan, who had been bayoneted, was unconscious. Naretena was still stunned from the blow from the musket. Tesalbestinay was calm. "Cochise will do something," she said.

Tahzay looked around the dim room. The only light came from a small window. He tried to straighten out in his mind what had happened. From as far back as he could remember his people and the Americans were friends. American soldiers had been kind men, men who joked and laughed and bought the Indian children candy at the trading post.

[85]

Culver and Walsh and Wallace were people he knew very well. Whenever they saw him they would stop what they were doing and talk with him.

But now all this was somehow changed. There had been words spoken in a tent and he had seen his father with a rage on him greater than any he had ever seen before and there had been violence and his cousin lay half dead on the floor with a bayonet gash on his side and his uncle was numbed from a blow — all done by these same American soldiers.

How did it happen so quickly? How could friends stop being friends so suddenly?

Tahzay was thirsty and hungry and tired and he felt very small and young. He was happy his mother was there with him. He wondered when his father would come to save them.

The Indians were given no food or water. During the night the wounded man groaned in pain. In the morning the prisoners rushed to the window at the sound of Cochise's voice. They saw him on the hilltop, and with him were two American captives.

"Wallace!" Cochise called out.

Buckley stepped out of the building and looked up the hill. "Stay here, Wallace," he said. "It's a trap."

"Let me go to him, Mr. Buckley," Wallace said. "I know Cochise. I can speak to him." Wallace walked to the wall of the corral.

"Wallace," Cochise said, "tell the white soldier boy I have two Americans to trade for my people."

Inside the storeroom, Tesalbestinay took Tahzay's hand. "They will make the exchange," she said. "All will be well."

Wallace returned to the building and told Lieutenant Bascom what Cochise had said.

"Tell him to release those white men or I'll hang the Indians!" Bascom said angrily.

Sergeant Bernard shook his head warningly. "Better make the trade, sir," he said. "I think you did wrong to try to arrest Cochise in the first place while you had a white flag flying."

"I am not interested in your opinion, Sergeant," Bascom said coldly. Then he looked again at Wallace. "Tell him to release his prisoners and return the Ward boy and then I'll free his relatives."

"I won't tell him that, Lieutenant," Wallace said. "I'm going out there and try to reason with him."

Wallace went outside the corral and walked up the hill. Cochise's first instinct was to greet him as the old friend he was. But then Cochise remembered that it was Wallace who had told him that Bascom wanted to see him. Suddenly the whole thing seemed to Cochise to have been a carefully prepared trap to get him into the hands of the white soldiers. He looked at Wallace harshly. "What does the boy soldier say?"

"I have come of my own free will," Wallace said. "I have come to ask you to release the prisoners you have here. Then maybe I can get the lieutenant to free your people."

"Is that what you have to say?" Cochise asked.

"The lieutenant says he wants the Ward boy."

[87]

Cochise's face filled with anger. "I do not have the child! No one of my people has the child. The soldier boy was the first one to take prisoners. He will be the first to free them."

"He will not do it," Wallace said.

"Then I will make you prisoner too. The soldier boy will want to make a trade then, maybe."

Cochise jerked his head to Nahilzay. Nahilzay threw a lariat over Wallace and trussed him up. Then the Indians and the American prisoners disappeared over the hill.

Tesalbestinay's face now was worried. A chill crept over her as she realized that matters were growing worse and not better.

The next day the station depot was surrounded by Indians. No one could leave a building without risking an Indian bullet. The days and nights passed. Water began to run low. Men and animals suffered. Juan's son was delirious. The Americans put a small amount of food and water in the storeroom each day but did not permit the prisoners to leave the room.

On the fifth day water ran out. The animals were getting frenzied. They could smell the water from the springs, some six hundred yards away. Finally Bascom ordered soldiers to take the animals to the springs and to fill up the water barrels. When the soldiers and animals reached the precious water, Indians, waiting in ambush, opened fire and drove the men back.

The following morning Cochise again appeared on the hilltop and, with Wallace speaking for him, again demanded that the prisoners be released. Bascom retorted that he would free the Indians when Cochise turned over the Ward child and the three Americans he held. Cochise swore that he knew nothing of the Ward boy. Bascom turned on his heel and went back into the building.

Two days later Sergeant Bernard led Lieutenant Bascom to one side of the corral and pointed to the hill. More than a hundred Apache warriors, in full war paint, were lined up on the summit. Seated on a horse in front of them, his face streaked with paint, his arms covered with beads and war amulets, was Cochise. Every man was loaded down with weapons.

Bascom was petrified. Now Cochise and his men looked the way he had imagined Indians should look. He could not believe that the man in the savage finery was the same near-naked tramp who had come to speak to him in the tent. As he stared in horror, Cochise shoved Wallace forward with a long spear. Wallace, a noose under his arms, stumbled a few yards down the stony hillside. Nahilzay paid out the lariat.

"Bascom!" Wallace called out in a hoarse voice.

"Yes!" the lieutenant shouted back.

"Can you hear me?"

"Yes."

"I can hardly talk," Wallace said. "I been freezing and I haven't had anything to eat. Listen, Bascom, this is the last chance. Cochise says he will let all of us go. The other two Americans are worse off than me. Cochise says if you let his relatives go he will let us go. He says this is the last time he will make the offer."

Lieutenant Bascom bit his lip. Then he saw Ward standing near him and his face hardened. "Tell Cochise to return the Ward boy with the three Americans and we will make the exchange."

"He says he hasn't got the Ward boy," Wallace said.

"Tell him I still say he is a liar!"

Now Sergeant Bernard spoke up. "Lieutenant, for God's sake, take him up. You will get three Americans for five Indians. That's plenty fair."

"I want the Ward boy as well," Bascom said.

"Sir, Cochise does not lie. Believe me. If he says he hasn't got the Ward boy, then he hasn't got him. For the love of God let those Indians go free and save the Americans while they're still alive or else there will be a real war on here."

Bascom pulled back his shoulder. His childish face became stern. "Cochise will have to learn who is in command in this country. If I gave in now we would never be able to control them."

"Lieutenant, listen to me," Bernard said earnestly. "I know these Indians. The other soldiers will agree with me. An Apache chief is not the supreme boss in his tribe. If any other warrior captured those white men he's got the right to do with them as he pleases, no matter what Cochise says. It's unusual to get this much bargaining and patience. I don't know how Cochise is holding back those fighting men of his, but for God's sake take him up before it's too late!"

Bascom hesitated for a moment and then he said: "I

came here to get the Ward boy. Those were my orders from the colonel. I am not going back without Mickey Free!"

Bernard lost his temper. "There are three white men whose lives are at stake!"

Bascom looked at Bernard icily. "Sergeant, I will thank you not to forget yourself. I was ordered to get the Ward boy and I will settle for nothing else."

"The hell with orders!" Bernard said furiously. "Those Indians will torture those men to death! You've never seen what's left of a man after they get through with him!"

Again Bascom hesitated and again Ward stepped up to his side. Now Bascom stood stiffly and said: "Sergeant Bernard, you are insubordinate. Consider yourself under arrest. I will prefer charges against you at a court-martial. I am in command here. Return to the building and remain inside until you receive further orders from me."

For several moments Bernard did not move and then his huge frame slumped. He saluted and walked to the building. Bascom now turned back to Wallace. "My offer still stands, Wallace. When Cochise stops lying and brings the Ward boy down his people will be freed. Not before."

Wallace held out his hands. "Please, Lieutenant!"

"I'm sorry, Wallace, but that's final." Bascom walked back into the building.

Naretena, standing at the window, said: "Now it is too late."

As the Indians watched from the window, Wallace suddenly tried to pull himself free. Nahilzay jerked him back.

The driver fell over and tried to cling to a rock. Nahilzay kicked his horse and pulled Wallace up the side of the hill. The driver, face down, was dragged helplessly.

Nahilzay, with a wild scream, raced his horse back and forth across the hilltop, pulling Wallace behind him like a sack of grain.

Naretena turned away from the window and prepared his mind for the death he knew was now inevitable.

A company of American soldiers found the three bodies of Cochise's prisoners in the now abandoned camp of the Chiricahua people. They brought the mutilated bodies to the Apache Pass station.

The Indian captives were taken from the storeroom. They were taken to where three other Indians, members of the Coyotero tribe captured by the newly-arrived soldiers, were standing. Tesalbestinay and Tahzay were separated from the others.

Naretena said quickly to Tahzay: "Tell Cochise that many must not suffer from the mistake of the child soldier."

The three Chiricahua Indians and the three Coyoteros were hanged from a great oak tree.

In the afternoon the sun blackened its face and the sky emptied its tears and the cloud birds threw rocks at each other. The wind spoke of its fury and then in the night the colliding of the sky rocks was noisy and brought out Lightning, who showed the mountain peaks against the sky, as though it were day, and with each brief visit from Lightning the six bodies could be seen swinging from the oak tree.

The wolves and the coyotes were silent in the storm and the storm also kept the sharp beaks of the buzzards away. When Cochise and Juan, with three chosen warriors — Nahilzay, Skinyea and Pionsenay — cut the bodies down they found them untouched. They buried the three Coyoteros and took their own dead back to the Stronghold.

The wife of Juan and the wives of his sons lay down and beat the earth. Cochise fired four shots into the air and then four again and four again. Cochise and Juan laid out the bodies and washed them and then painted the faces red and yellow so they would look well for the journey. They dressed them in their best clothing and then buried them with their heads to the west.

The people sorrowed for twenty days. No one spoke to Cochise except Nahilzay, who brought him the news that Tesalbestinay and Tahzay had returned safely to the camp. On the twenty-first day Cochise called Nochalo. The shaman threw some ghost powder into the fire. The powder made great clouds of black smoke.

On the following day Cochise called his warriors together. In slow speech he repeated everything that had happened. The words came from his lips like drippings of ice. The moon was rising as he spoke the first words and it was far across the sky before he finished. When he was done he removed his red turban and put it on the ground. He raised his arms stiffly. He lifted his face to the sky. He said: "There will be war to the death with the white-eyes!

[93]

There will be ten white-eyes slain for every Indian slain! This I pledge! This I pledge!"

Nochalo stepped into the firelight. With two holy medicine sticks he lifted the red turban from the ground without touching it with his hands and put it back on Cochise's head. Cochise said again: "Ten white-eyes will die for every Indian who is killed! This I pledge!"

Men began to beat on rawhide drums and the warriors chanted their song of battle.

For four nights the dancing and singing continued and then Cochise sent a messenger to Mangas Coloradas, inviting him to join forces with him. Then fires were lighted on the tops of mountain peaks, calling other Apache tribes to a war of extermination against the Americans.

When the courier was gone and the fires were lighted, Cochise took his son, Tahzay, and brought him to the grave of Naretena, and there both father and son lay down on the earth and wept.

CHAPTER IX

Captain Thomas Jeffords touched his fingers to his forehead in informal salute. "You sent for me, General?" he
asked. He took a large kerchief from his pocket and wiped
his face.

It was a hot day in the summer of 1862. The Civil War
had been raging for more than a year. At the start of hos-
tilities, the tall, red-bearded prospector had offered his serv-
ices to the Union Army, and since no man excelled him in
his knowledge of the country and the ways of Indians, he
was taken on eagerly as a government scout. A few days
before, he had received word that General Edward R. S.
Canby, in command of the Department of New Mexico,
wanted to see him at his headquarters at Fort Thorn, near
La Cruces. Jeffords hastened there immediately.

General Canby, a wiry, bearded officer, bit off the end

of a stogie. He pushed the box of cigars toward Jeffords. "I want you to go to Tucson on a mission for me, Tom," he said abruptly.

Jeffords selected a cigar. He lit it. "All right," he said. "When do you want me to leave?"

Canby puffed hard on the stogie. "Not so fast, young man. The way you talk you'd think there were no Apaches between here and Tucson. Do you know what's been going on in Apacheria?"

"I've heard that Cochise is acting up," Jeffords said.

"Acting up? I wish he were just acting up!" Canby said forcefully. "Cochise has started a full-scale war!"

"Maybe you'd better fill me in, sir," Jeffords said. He sat down. The heat in the room was intense.

Canby leaned forward earnestly. "Tom, there has never been anything like this before. Cochise has gathered together all the Apache tribes. For the first time in years the Apaches have stopped fighting among themselves and are concentrating on fighting the white man."

Jeffords nodded. "I heard that some second lieutenant touched it off."

"I'm afraid that's true, Tom," Canby admitted. "He dealt very foolishly with Cochise in a matter that was of very small importance. And it doesn't help to know that Cochise was telling the complete truth. It was something about a half-breed child who was kidnaped. It turned out that another tribe of Indians was responsible, not the Chiricahuas. But it was too late then." Canby sighed. "I do not want to say anything against Bascom, the officer involved.

[96]

He was killed gallantly at the Battle of Val Verde. Let his bones rest in peace.

"But things have worked out very well for Cochise. It would have been a problem at any time. But now this war with the South is playing right into his hands. Last June Fort Buchanan was ordered abandoned by the War Department. All its stores were destroyed. Its garrison of some 500 men were removed for action in the east. Cochise figured that this was a kind of surrender. He thinks it is his warfare that has caused the fort to be abandoned."

General Canby got up and walked to a large map on the wall. Jeffords followed him.

"Fort Breckenridge also was ordered abandoned," Canby continued, pointing to the map. "The country out there is entirely without military protection. Cochise is having a field day. He thinks the army is afraid to stand up to him. Blood is flowing everywhere. The Butterfield stations are abandoned. The line is out. Ranchers have fled from their homes. Homesteaders have been killed — the rest have left everything behind. People who managed to escape with their lives have flocked to Tucson and Tubac.

"The Apaches are merciless. They kill everyone they can get their hands on. There isn't a place on the desert that isn't covered with charred wagons, bodies, bleached bones. Apache Pass where the Bascom business took place is the worst place of all. I'm told that one is almost able to walk from one end of the pass to the other without having to touch the ground — so thick are the wagons and skeletons of the victims!"

Canby began to pace up and down the office, his hands behind his back. Smoke trailed behind him. "If I seem to sound melodramatic, Tom, believe me when I say that I have not begun to tell all I know. The Apaches are fighting as a single army, under a single command: Cochise. And Cochise is fighting so skillfully my great regret is that he is not fighting on our side. The man is a military genius! The Apaches attack in forces as high as two or three hundred at a time. They roam the country, striking everywhere." He paused and looked at Jeffords. "They even laid siege to Tucson! And they quit only when they were good and ready!"

Canby seemed to lose himself in his thoughts. Then he said: "Now, about Tucson. When the war started between the States, there seem to have been exactly sixty-eight native-born Americans in the place. These people convened, and voted to join the Confederacy. Last August, Lieutenant Colonel Baylor, a Rebel commander of Mounted Rifles, issued a proclamation establishing the Territory of Arizona for the South. He appointed himself governor."

Jeffords whistled silently.

"Five months ago, in January, Baylor sent two hundred Rebel soldiers to Tucson to take over the place. He might still own the place if it were not for General James Carleton and his California Column. Carleton marched from California at the head of his army of volunteers and Baylor fled from Tucson before Carleton got there. I received all this information from a Rebel prisoner we captured.

"As far as I know, Tom, Carleton is still in command at

Tucson. He has tried to get in touch with me, I understand, but all his couriers were intercepted by Indians or the Rebs." Canby paused and looked at Jeffords. "That's where you come in, Tom. I must know how strong Carleton's forces are. How well they are equipped. Everything I plan to do from this end depends on what's happening over there. If Carleton is strong enough I can plan on a campaign to drive the Rebels out of New Mexico. If he is not strong — then maybe he will need assistance from me to hold on to what he's got. I cannot move without knowing the exact situation in Tucson."

Canby walked over to the map again and stared at it. "Between here and Tucson lies the heart of the Apache country. I will not *order* you to make this journey."

Jeffords knocked the ashes from his cigar. "I asked you before, General — when do you want me to leave? You haven't answered yet."

Canby grinned. "Do you want an escort, Tom?"

"No."

"I want you to go immediately," Canby said.

It was almost a week later when Thomas Jeffords saw at last the high edifice of the Catholic church in Tucson. He breathed heavily in his relief. Although he had seen no Indians on the trail from Las Cruces, he had seen Indian signs everywhere. He had traveled swiftly and carefully, picking up pony prints on the hard desert, seeing Indian smoke signals. With his profound knowledge of the country he had taken secret paths he had learned about during his years as a prospector. Although not a shot had been fired at him, he saw the outline of the church in the distance with vast cheer. He spurred his weary horse and soon entered the walled Old Pueblo of Tucson.

He drew up before General Carleton's headquarters and presented himself immediately to the general. Carleton, a tall, energetic man, looked at the travel-stained man who stood before him and asked impatiently: "What do you want?"

"I have just come from General Canby, sir," Jeffords said.

"Canby? From New Mexico?"

"Yes, sir."

Carleton stood up in astonishment. "Do you mean that you have crossed Apacheria?"

"Yes, sir."

Carleton's amazement was so great he could not speak. "But how could you?" he asked at last. "I've lost half a dozen men trying to get word to General Canby." Then he rushed around the desk and took the hand of Jefford and pumped it. "I'm proud to shake your hand," he said. "I was beginning to believe nobody could get by Cochise!"

"I was lucky," Jeffords said laconically.

"Sit down, sir, sit down," Carleton said. "You must be exhausted." When Jeffords was comfortably seated, Carleton said: "And now, sir, what is it that General Canby desires me to know?"

Jeffords handed Carleton papers which identified him as a courier from Canby, and when Carleton finished looking at them, he told the general what Canby had said. As he spoke, Carleton's eyes began to sparkle. When Jeffords finished, the general pounded his fist on the desk.

"That is excellent news, Captain Jeffords," he said in a ringing voice. "We have complete control of the territory here. As far as the Rebs are concerned, that is. There is nothing to prevent the California Column from going on east to join General Canby."

"Nothing except Cochise," Jeffords commented.

"I think our army can fight off even Cochise!"

"General Canby will be happy to lay eyes on you."

"I've already sent out a detachment of men to set up camp on San Simon. They had trouble with Apaches going through Apache Pass but they got through. My idea was to have a strong point between Tucson and the Rio Grande, stocked with food and supplies, so if we were ordered to join General Canby the main body of troops could travel as lightly as possible. Now that I know what General Canby wants, I shall send out additional supplies and establish more camps on the way, and then as rapidly as possible I shall follow up with the remainder of the troops."

"With your permission, sir, I will start back immediately and tell General Canby what your plans are."

"You can travel with the detachment, Captain Jeffords."

"Good. When will they leave?"

"How much rest do you need?"

"A bath. A night's sleep. A bath more than anything."

Carleton rubbed his hands in satisfaction. "I will give orders for the detachment to make ready as quickly as possible." He looked soberly at Jeffords. "You have performed an important service for your country, Captain Jeffords. I will mention you in my dispatches. I do not believe any other man could have crossed Apacheria as you did."

Several hours later, bathed, his clothing cleaned, Jeffords strolled down the streets of the Old Pueblo, puffing contentedly on a cigar. He was surprised when a pleasant-looking, slender man waved to him. "You are Captain Jeffords, are you not?"

"I believe you have the advantage of me, sir," Jeffords replied.

"My name is St. John. We met at Mesilla, some years ago. I worked for the Butterfield people then."

Jeffords smiled broadly and extended his hand. "Of course. How are you?"

"Very well, thank you. Have you just arrived?"

"Got in this morning."

"Are you bound for a drink?"

"That sounds like an excellent idea!"

"Let's go to the Congress Hall, Captain Jeffords. It's right across the way."

The saloon was large and well-filled. Soldiers and civilians leaned against the long bar. Other men played cards at small tables. St. John led the way to a table in a corner of the room. The men ordered drinks.

"What have you been doing since we last met?" St. John asked.

"A little of everything. Mostly prospecting — until the war started. Then I started to scout for the Union."

"What brings you to Tucson?"

"I carried some dispatches to General Carleton." Jeffords swallowed his drink. "Is the Butterfield Line out for good, Mr. St. John?"

"I'm afraid so."

"That's too bad. This country needs communication."

St. John toyed with his glass. "We were doing quite well. The Indians — in the Chiricahua country at least — were friendly. Civil War or not, it might be a different story if it were not for the terrible episode in Apache Pass."

"Bascom?"

"Yes. The tragedy of it is that Bascom never realized how wrong he was. And the army backed him up. You know he received a commendation for what he did." St. John sighed. "Ah, well, there is no use going over that. Only I often wonder how different the history of the Southwest might have been if Bascom had been a wiser man."

"Have you ever met Cochise?" Jeffords asked suddenly.

"Yes."

"Tell me about him."

"It's a curious thing, Captain Jeffords, but when I first met him I thought of you."

"Of me?" Jeffords said in surprise.

"I remembered what you had told me in Mesilla that time. You know — about how the Indians should be treated as human beings. Cochise? He is an unusual man, Captain

Jeffords. I believe he is a great man. It is tragic that his wisdom and leadership are being directed against us."

The following day Jeffords reported back to Carleton. He found the general with a young, clean-shaven officer. Both men were poring over a military map. Carleton looked up with a smile when Jeffords entered his office.

"Are you ready to start back, Captain Jeffords?" he asked.

"Yes, sir."

"Excellent! Captain Jeffords, this is Captain Thomas Roberts, in command of E Company, First California Dragoons." Jeffords and the captain shook hands. "Roberts is going to bring supplies to San Simon," Carleton continued. "I will follow up with some two thousand men to strengthen General Canby's forces. Jeffords, you will accompany Roberts as far as San Simon and then continue on to New Mexico."

"Very good, General," Jeffords said.

"Captain Roberts will be in command. More troops will join him at a place on the San Pedro. You are not a regular member of the armed forces, Captain Jeffords, but it is necessary that you consider yourself under Captain Roberts's command. On the other hand, Captain, Jeffords knows the country well and he also knows Indians. I suggest you listen to his advice."

Roberts gave Jeffords a friendly smile. "We will have no trouble between us, sir," he said.

The troops of E Company, with thirty wagons loaded with supplies, formed in the plaza. The day was broiling.

The soldiers were in full uniform and carried heavy packs. Looking at the men, Jeffords thought their outfits were much too heavy for a desert march. He thought of how Apache fighting men traveled, with not an ounce of waste equipment on them.

Included in the weapons were two twelve-pound mountain howitzers. Jeffords looked at these weapons, novel in that part of the country, with interest.

"We brought them all the way from California," Roberts said proudly. "Might have some use for them sometime."

The plaza was filled with spectators, most of them Mexican, since until less than ten years before the Old Pueblo had been a part of Mexico. Roberts signaled to the bugler and when the high, piercing notes cut across the open space, the men and women cheered and waved their hands. The drummer started the beat, and with General Carleton taking the salute, the troops marched out of the city.

The soldiers tramped through the blazing day. At four o'clock in the afternoon Jeffords pointed out pony prints. A little later he saw some horse droppings. He examined them. He studied a patch of trampled grass. He broke off a blade and felt for the moisture in it.

"Indians?" Roberts asked.

"About twenty of them," Jeffords said. "They passed here maybe four or five hours ago — maybe a little less. They know about us." He walked over to a small pile of stones, laid out in a straight line, with other stones arranged to make an arrow, pointed east. "Seems they have our plans figured," Jeffords said. "The stones say a company of men are headed for the Chiricahuas."

"What do you suggest?" Roberts asked.

Jeffords straightened out. "You can see for miles in this country. No use trying to travel in secret — not with a force this big. But I think we're strong enough so they won't try to jump us."

The march was resumed. At sunset the troop halted for a brief rest, and then Roberts ordered them on. They marched through the night, and shortly after dawn reached the first camp in the abandoned Butterfield station on the San Pedro where a cavalry troop, under the command of Captain John Cremony, was waiting for them.

The men rested through the day while the officers planned the next stage. Roberts said: "It is twenty-eight miles to Dragoon Springs. The question is whether there is enough water there to supply both Captain Cremony's men and my own, at the same time, plus all the animals. Or whether we should divide forces again and plan to arrive at the springs separately. What is your opinion, Captain Jeffords?"

"It's a dry time now," Jeffords said. "Maybe you ought to split up."

"I believe I will do that," Roberts agreed. "I will go ahead with my infantry, Captain Cremony. I'll take some of your mounted men for scouts."

Again the men set out.

CHAPTER X

When Tom Jeffords had interpreted the meaning of the arrow made of stones to Captain Roberts he had been entirely correct.

From the moment the American soldiers marched out of Tucson, they were under the watchful eye of Cochise. The spies reported to the Indian chief the exact number of the soldiers and the number of the wagons loaded with supplies.

By means of signal fires, Cochise was informed of the direction of the march. He knew when the troops stopped on the San Pedro. When he learned that they moved on east from there he knew they had to go to Dragoon Springs for water — and then, on to the water in Apache Pass.

The wily Chiricahua leader decided to lay ambush in Apache Pass. With its series of interlocking hills and canyons, its rocky caves and ravines, Apache Pass provided a superb place for surprise attack.

For this occasion, Cochise planned something bigger than an ordinary ambush. From bitter experience he had learned to respect the accuracy and the firing power of the American guns. He decided this time to do more than just drive the soldiers off and capture their supplies. He planned to trap all of them — to kill as many as he could — to inflict upon the hated soldiers the greatest defeat in his campaign against them.

While the weary troops were plodding across the blazing desert, Cochise had his warriors build a number of stone barricades in the hills above the springs in the pass. While these breastworks were being constructed he went down to the springs again and again and looked up at them to make sure they could not be seen from below.

The work, backbreaking in the intense heat, made many of the Apache fighting men grumble. This kind of preparation was unusual in Indian warfare. Nahilzay, his eyes flaming with battle fever, urged that Cochise forget his plans to lie still and wait for the Americans to come to him.

"Let us attack them at dawn, in the usual fashion, while they sleep," Nahilzay said. "It is the way of the Apache!"

Since the Bascom affair the Chiricahua leader seemed to have aged ten years. His face was lined and his hair was streaked with gray and his body carried new scars. He listened to Nahilzay and then he replied harshly: "Your temper has not cooled and you will not learn. I have tried to teach you, but you still believe each attack is the same as the one before it. The Americans know about what you call 'the way of the Apache.' They are prepared for that way. They will not be prepared for this."

While the work was going on a messenger arrived from Mangas Coloradas. The Mimbres chief besought Cochise to join him in fighting against American miners in New Mexico. Cochise shook his head. "Return to your leader," he said to the courier. "Tell Mangas Coloradas that if he wants battle to join me here in Apache Pass."

A sudden unexpected storm struck the desert. The rain came down in torrents. The soldiers plowed through the miserable weather. The ground became like soft clay, clinging to their boots, making their feet feel as though they were weighted with lead.

In the early hours of the morning of July 15, 1862, the soldiers reached Dragoon Springs. Roberts sent a rider back to Cremony with orders for him to bring on the cavalry and the supplies. Cremony arrived at Dragoon Springs at three that same afternoon.

Still worried that there would be insufficient water in Apache Pass for both companies at once, Roberts set out again at 5:30 in the afternoon, instructing Cremony to take to the saddle at dawn the next day. The infantrymen trudged through the night. The sun broke early and hot the next morning. The men staggered on, beaten by the brassy fire from above.

Just before eight o'clock in the morning they reached one of the abandoned Butterfield depots and briefly rested. Then Roberts gave the order to move again.

The heat was such as no man had ever before experienced. The soldiers were not like troops on march. They looked more like a defeated, broken army, after battle. They churned through the scorching sands. One after the other, men collapsed. Precious water was used to revive them. Other soldiers divided the gear of the stricken men to lighten their loads.

Into the murderous heat the men drove themselves. Dry dust filled their throats like bits of fire. Their eyes burned and watered and the straps of their kits cut into their backs like sharp knives.

By noon, despite Captain Roberts's orders to conserve water, the canteens were almost empty. The men moved on, their throats like sandpaper. They watched the ball of fire in the sky with fascinated eyes and counted each inch the sun slipped toward the rim of the mountains in the west.

From his hiding place high on the hill at the western entrance to Apache Pass, Cochise watched the soldiers approach. In the clear air, his eyes, keen as an eagle's, saw the dust of the marching more than twenty-five miles away. He waited, quietly, patiently, his eyes glittering, as the dust cloud grew larger. His warriors were ready. Each man was in his place. The Indians were rested from their labors. And Cochise knew what condition the soldiers would be in after the desert march.

While the Apaches waited, a band of warriors under the command of Mangas Coloradas arrived from the east. The two chiefs greeted each other, and then Mangas Coloradas asked: "Why did my brother refuse to join me in my war against the miners?"

For answer, Cochise pointed to the west. He said: "Soldiers. From Tucson. With many wagons of supplies." Then Cochise showed Mangas Coloradas the preparations he had made to ambush the soldiers. The Mimbres leader was deeply impressed. "Join me here," Cochise said. "Then we will attack the miners in New Mexico later."

Mangas Coloradas agreed instantly. He placed his men under the orders of Cochise. Cochise disposed of them among his own warriors waiting behind the stone barricades. Mangas Coloradas then joined Cochise to await the soldiers.

While they were waiting a scout dashed up to them with the news that thirteen Americans were approaching the pass from the east. When he described their appearance, Mangas Coloradas grunted: "I recognize the description. They are miners from Santa Rita del Cobre."

"Enju," Cochise said impassively. "You wanted to fight miners."

"These men are dangerous," Mangas Coloradas said. "They are always well armed, and they are experienced fighters. It may be that they will interfere with your plans."

"They never will enter the pass," Cochise said. He glanced westward again. The soldiers were still a long way off. He called to Tahzay and asked him to select twenty warriors. Then he mounted a pony and bade Mangas Coloradas come with them.

The band rode swiftly to the east mouth of Apache Pass. Several miles away they could make out the little group of miners. Cochise said: "From the moment these men enter the pass they will be alert. It is the wise thing to attack them before they reach the pass."

"That is open country," Mangas Coloradas said. "How can you surprise them out there?"

"It is Chiricahua country," Cochise said. "Tahzay!"

The son of Cochise, who now was a strong and brave warrior, said: "Yes, Father."

"What lies a short distance to the east of the pass?"

"A gully," Tahzay said instantly.

"What of this gully?"

"We marked it before, for just such a time," Tahzay said. "It is deep to the height of a man and its length would shelter a hundred warriors. It cannot be seen by a man on a horse until he is almost on it."

Cochise nodded with grim satisfaction. "Is it necessary to give you orders, my son? Or instructions?"

"No, Father."

"Then show my brother from the Mimbres people how Chiricahuas make the earth fight for them!"

As Mangas Coloradas watched, Tahzay and the warriors he had chosen stripped themselves of everything except breechclouts and moccasins. Then they rolled in the thick alkali dirt. They stood up, covered with a gray film, their

[112]

painted bodies and faces now a neutral color that blended perfectly with the desert.

Without further word from Cochise, they scampered away silently, their guns at their sides, and a few moments later they disappeared from sight.

The miners came closer. Their rifles were still in the saddle scabbards. Their pistols were in holsters. They looked around the unbroken, open country on all sides of them. They were confident and careless in the flat land where they could see a desert rabbit running a quarter of a mile away.

When they reached a point a few yards away from the gully the hidden Apaches opened fire on them. Six of the miners fell dead in the first volley. The others, in panic from the gunfire which seemed to come from the earth itself, tried to defend themselves against an enemy they could not see. They were cut down before they could fire a shot.

Tahzay and his men came out of their concealment and gathered in the horses and stripped the dead men of their weapons and ammunition. Tahzay found a leather pouch on one man filled with gold dust to the value of fifty thousand dollars.

Cochise smiled as he looked at the pop-eyed Mangas Coloradas. "Now for the soldiers," he said.

In the early afternoon, Roberts and his men came to the mouth of Apache Pass. The soldiers now were moving like sleepwalkers. The heat and thirst had robbed them of decision. They slipped on small stones and regained their balance with difficulty. Their necks and wrists were chafed and bleeding from the rubbing of their uniforms.

Roberts called a halt at the entrance to the pass and sent some mounted scouts into the opening to investigate. Jeffords studied the pass through binoculars. Shadows already crossed its steep slopes and in contrast to the other places the dark parts were almost black. It looked cool and quiet. A slight breeze drifted out of the pass and the men gulped the cool air as though it were water.

Jeffords felt a slight uneasiness he could not explain.

"The place seems almost too quiet," he said to Roberts.

"If it's empty, there's no reason it shouldn't be quiet, is there?" Roberts asked.

"I reckon not," Jeffords said. But he could not shake off the feeling.

The scouts returned and reported that the pass was empty. Roberts looked questioningly at Jeffords. The prospector shook his head. "I guess I'm just tired," he said. "I keep seeing things that aren't there."

Captain Roberts gave the order to march into the pass.

The men walked silently. They looked around, wearily, their rifles in hand. They thought of the water that waited ahead. The breeze came cooler. And then from the hills of both sides of the pass came a barrage of bullets and arrows.

"Sound retreat!" Roberts shouted immediately to the bugler. He prayed that the exhausted soldiers would have enough discipline to respond, that they would not become wild and panic-stricken because of their thirst and the fact that the water was being denied to them. Then Roberts said: "Thank God, thank God," as the soldiers obeyed instantly, firing at the invisible Indians, moving back away from the water, back into the open valley.

The men were soldiers now. The heat and the long march were forgotten. "We've got to get back in there," Roberts said tersely. "We can't march back those forty miles without water." The captain summoned Jeffords to his side. "Is there any way to the water except through the pass entrance?"

"None that I know of, Captain," Jeffords replied.

"Then we have to go in through the front door!"

"You might try sending skirmishers over the hills to try to get behind the Indians," Jeffords suggested.

"It was a beautiful ambush," Roberts said.

"Cochise," Jeffords murmured, looking into the pass.

Roberts sent out skirmishers and then he sent a small detachment of soldiers into the mouth of the pass to draw the Indian fire.

Tahzay slithered around rocks until he was at the side of his father. "The soldiers have something I have never seen before," he said. He pointed. "There — those men are pulling it."

Cochise looked down at the mountain howitzers on their carriages. He frowned. "I have never seen such things either," he said.

"Nor have I," said Mangas Coloradas.

[115]

The skirmishers sent up behind the Indians reached the summit of the hill and opened fire and at the same time Roberts ordered a barrage laid on from below. Caught between both fires, the Indians fought back ferociously. They retreated gradually until, late in the afternoon, Roberts finally got his men to the old Butterfield station in the pass, and there they took shelter behind the corral walls.

Now Cochise ordered the Indians to get behind the barricades built above the springs. "The soldiers have reached the station," he said to Mangas Coloradas. "But they are still a long way from water."

The stage depot provided protection for the soldiers from Indian attack; but as Cochise had said, they were still without the vital water. The springs were so close — and yet were as far as they had ever been. Night was falling. The men had marched for twenty-two hours across the desert and then had fought a bitter battle for more than five hours.

After the smallest of rests, Roberts ordered his men to try to get to the springs. They moved silently in the twilight. Then, when the sound of the water was clear in their ears, they were subjected to a blazing barrage from the Indians stationed in their strong points above. The muskets of the soldiers, firing into the deep shadows of the canyon walls, were useless against the protected Indians.

Jeffords crept away and ran swiftly, catlike, up the hill to the right of the springs. He crouched behind a rock and watched for several minutes and then he returned to Roberts. "Those Indians are not scattered around above the springs the way they were spread out at the pass entrance," he said. "Their fire is coming in concentrated bursts. They must have built themselves some kind of protection out of stones."

"The howitzers," Roberts said instantly.

"Musket fire is useless," Jeffords agreed. "But if you can land howitzer shells in the right places you'll be able to kill them in bunches!"

Roberts ordered the howitzers brought into position. "Hold your fire until I give the orders," he said to the gunners. "Study the Indian fire. Determine exactly where it is coming from. Then, when I give the word — *make every shell count!*"

One howitzer was placed to fire on the north wall; the other on the south. Roberts ordered the soldiers to open up with their muskets. There was an immediate response from the Indians. Then Roberts gave the word to the men at the cannon to let go.

The gun on the left found its target with the first shot. There was a shattering explosion on the side of the hill — followed by a great outcry of pain and surprise from the Indians.

The gun on the right was less well handled. Unaccountably it was overturned. The men handling it were driven away by Indian fire. Jeffords called for volunteers. With six men he ran to the gun. Under the most concentrated fire, they managed to right it again and turn it on the Indians.

At that moment, a burst of fire revealed an Indian enclosure. The howitzer was fired. The shell found its target.

Now both field pieces had the range. They fired shell

after shell into the hills. The air was filled with the savage screams of pain and terror from the Indians. Then, just before the last light departed, the soldiers saw Indians fleeing in all directions.

They were too exhausted, too parched, to shout their victory. The canyon was silent. The men staggered to the springs and fell on their bellies and put their faces into the cool water.

CHAPTER XI

After the soldiers continued on their way to New Mexico, the Indians returned to the springs to collect their dead. Cochise looked bitterly at the destruction which had been wrought by the howitzers. He looked at the shattered boulders. At the gaping holes. At the dead bodies and pieces of bodies which lay everywhere.

"It did not work," Mangas Coloradas said in his deep voice.

"They were defeated," Cochise replied fiercely. "Until they used the fire-wagons, they were defeated."

"But they used the fire-wagons," Mangas Coloradas said. He watched his own warriors collect the Mimbres dead. "Apaches were not meant to hide behind rocks when they fight."

Chochise nodded heavily. "You are right, my brother. A defeat is not so terrible a thing if something can be learned from it. My own warriors did not want to fight this way. The blame is all my own."

Mangas Coloradas touched him on the arm. "There were victories enough before. There will be victories again."

When the bodies were counted it was revealed that sixty-three Apaches had been killed and many more wounded. It was the worst defeat the Indians had ever suffered in a single battle. There were those, Cochise knew, who would die of their wounds, and others who would never fight again.

When the last man had been buried and Mangas Coloradas had taken his warriors away, Cochise brought his people into the Stronghold. News of the shattering defeat had preceded them and the women were waiting silently. The silence changed rapidly into a chorus of mourning that filled the Stronghold from one end to the other.

Wherever Cochise walked he saw faces seared with sorrow. His people turned from him as he walked among them. His brain felt as though it were on fire. He needed his people now — but he could not reach out to them.

There was no one he could talk to. Tahzay was a youth with intelligence, but he was a youth still, without memory or experience to give his words depth. Nahilzay, Juan, Skinyea, Pionsenay — brave warriors all — but not men with whom he could hold counsel. He needed his dead brother, Naretena, he thought with bitterness.

The sorrow penetrated his own wickiup. Tahzay, wounded slightly from flying stones after a shell burst, was silent, and Cochise saw with sadness that the smooth, beloved body of his son now was beginning to collect its own scars — scars, he thought, the mark of the Apache.

Tesalbestinay placed food before her husband. He was without appetite. The food tasted like ashes. He said at last: "Speak, woman. I know your tongue is heavy with words."

"Listen to the mourning of your people, Cochise," Tesalbestinay said. "It is speech enough."

"Battles have been lost before," he said in a dull voice.

"Listen! The cries of the women are like the wind."

He bowed his head silently.

"Let the sound reach your heart," she said. Then she fell on her knees before him and took his hand. "It is not too late to undo. There is food in our homes. There are weapons and fine horses. There is even yellow iron."

"It is too late," he said in a voice that seemed to come from out of the earth.

"It will be too late only when no Chiricahua man is alive," she said. "It is not too late, Cochise."

He stood up suddenly and walked out of the wickiup. He gestured for Tahzay to follow him. The father and son walked to a small rise. Cochise seated himself on a rock. The sun was far to the west. He lifted his arms to the sun and asked for guidance and then he said to Tahzay: "What thought is in your head, my son?"

Tahzay waited a long time before he replied. This was

the first time his father had honored him by asking for his advice. "From the beginning, I remember that you taught me it was the destiny of the Indian to make peace with the white man," he said finally. "Nothing has happened to make that less true. The battle at Apache Pass made that more true than ever."

"You are right, my son," Cochise said. "I believed then that that was the right thing for the Indian — and I do not say that I do not believe it now. But where can a man go to make such a peace? What white man has the power to agree to peace — and the power to keep it among his own people? What white man has honor that I can trust?"

Tahzay shook his young head. "I do not know."

"I do not know either," Cochise said. "Other Indian leaders have tried to make peace with the white man. They have sat down to speak with Americans — and they were poisoned where they sat. Less than three moons ago white men called together many Indians to a meeting to make peace and had guns waiting while they sat down — and all the Indians were killed."

"Yes," Tahzay said. "It is not easy."

Cochise looked at the dying sun. "It is death either way, maybe. What have my people done to bring this upon them? Is it better to die fighting — or to die seeking peace?"

Tahzay said: "Perhaps my father could find a white man with honor if he turned his mind on seeking such a man."

Cochise turned slowly to his son. He put his hand on

his shoulder and his fingers tightened. "I will seek such a man," he said.

In the night the snow fell. From the center of the domed roofs of the wickiups, thin trails of smoke twisted upward. The Apaches huddled in their Chiricahua Mountains. For six months Cochise had kept his people quiet while he tried to find some way to get together with a responsible American with whom he could talk about ending the war.

The skin door of the wickiup opened and Delgadito, a lieutenant to Mangas Coloradas, entered. He seated himself silently.

After a pause, Cochise asked: "How does it fare with my brother, Mangas Coloradas?"

Delgadito replied: "He is dead."

Tesalbestinay, making a new pair of moccasins for Cochise, stopped in her work, bone needle in one hand, deerskin in the other.

"He was an old man, filled with many years," Cochise said.

"He did not die of his years," Delgadito said.

"He was ever in the forefront of battle."

"He did not die in battle."

Tesalbestinay, sister to Mangas Coloradas, leaned forward. "How did my brother die?"

"He was invited into an American military camp under a white flag by an American general. When he arrived there he was made prisoner. While he was bound he was shot in the back by American soldiers and then he was beheaded."

"He went to this camp freely?" Cochise asked, suddenly hoarse.

"He went freely, and under guarantee of safety," Delgadito said. "Within three hours he was dead."

For a long while there was silence in the wickiup and then Cochise said: "Return to your people."

Delgadito asked: "How can he be buried when the Americans have his body?"

Cochise pondered.

"How will he make the journey to the dark place if he is not buried properly?" Delgadito asked. "Among us there is no one who can answer this question."

Cochise said: "Place his possessions in a cave and go through the ceremony. It will be as though he himself were there."

Delgadito left. Cochise said to Tesalbestinay: "The white men will not have peace."

Tesalbestinay crawled toward him and pressed her face on the earth. Her hands found her husband's ankles and she held them tightly — as though she feared slipping away. "We are the same now, husband," she said. "We have each lost a brother to the white-eyes and we are the same."

He touched her head gently. "Cry," he said.

"I cannot."

"Cry," he repeated softly.

"I have forgotten how to cry."

"There is no ending," he said. "There are only beginnings, always beginnings."

She lifted her dry-eyed face to him. "Will it be the same — an empty grave, with only the things he owned and touched?"

Cochise shook his head slowly. "It will not be the same."

During the next few weeks Cochise isolated himself and spent many hours in meditation. He tried to make himself understand what was happening. It did not seem possible to him that men who fought as bravely as the Americans could be so treacherous. But the events everywhere spoke for themselves and could not be denied.

Less than a month after Mangas Coloradas was slain by American soldiers, a delegation of Mimbres warriors presented themselves to Cochise. They informed him that a chief named Victorio had been chosen as the new leader of the Mimbres Apaches and that it was the desire of the Mimbres warriors that Cochise take over the war leadership of the Mimbres tribe.

After he listened to the speakers, Cochise said: "We will join our forces. But I tell you this: our cause is lost."

"We will destroy all Americans!" one of the warriors cried.

Cochise shook his head. "Together we will last a little longer, maybe," he said. "But in the end we will lose."

"With both our peoples fighting together we can drive the white-eyes from the land," another warrior shouted.

"It is not so," Cochise said wearily. "Our time is passing. Other people have passed by and have left markings on stones. We have left nothing on the stones. The forests will grow and the rivers will flow and the sun will heat our earth — but there will be nothing of us."

The men looked at him silently.

"No, we will leave no markings on stones, and no empty dwellings in the cliffs to show that once we were a people and lived here upon the earth." Cochise now raised his clenched fists and his voice grew harsh. "But we will leave behind us bones — and memories — and when we are gone we will take with us many of our enemies for companions.

"It will be said of us that no one fought more bravely than the Apache! It will be said that no one held out longer against the foe! I will be your leader. Henceforth you are to me the same as my own people. But we are doomed — and we join hands with that knowledge."

The Mimbres chieftans swore fealty to Cochise and pledged themselves to follow him to the death.

"It will not change things," Cochise said. "But it is better for us to die together. And when we are gone there will be a great hole where we stood, and in this emptiness there will echo again and again: APACHE!"

CHAPTER XII

The long train of covered wagons moved slowly along the rocky trail. Tom Jeffords rode up and down the length of the train and passed the word to the drivers: "Keep close, men. This is Apache country."

And it looked like Apache country, the red-bearded man thought. The earth itself seemed filled with hatred for the white man. And from time to time there was plainer evidence of the enmity of Cochise: the bones and the graves and the burned wreckage of wagons that had tried to pass before.

It was in the late fall of 1865, six months after the end of the Civil War. A few weeks before, Jeffords had been released from his duties as government scout. He had rested briefly in Mesilla, New Mexico Territory, and then he had agreed to lead a wagon train coming from Kansas and bound for California through Apacheria to Tucson.

"Keep close," he repeated to the drivers of the wagons. "Keep your guns handy."

His keen eyes surveyed the country alertly. From now until the walled city of Tucson was reached, the travelers were in their greatest danger. The train was large and the men were well armed. Jeffords did not think it likely that Apaches would attack the whole train. But he knew the wily Indians were past masters at picking off strays — cutting off wagons that became separated from others.

Cochise now dominated the entire Arizona Territory. He used his men and resources in a matchless manner. The domain of the Indian leader stretched from the Mimbres country in New Mexico almost all the way to California, and from the Gila River as far south as he cared to send his warriors.

The Apache chief had become a living legend of death and horror. From time to time he was reported dead, insane, wounded, deposed. He proved constantly that he was none of these things. He scattered his warriors throughout the land he claimed as his own and used them as savage shock troops. He had abandoned the large-sized battles — such as the one that had proved so disastrous in Apache Pass. Big battles with big concentrations of men was the white man's war. Cochise made the white man fight his kind of war: sudden early-morning raids, followed by quick retreats. Against this kind of warfare the soldiers were virtually helpless. In groups of twenty and thirty and forty the

Apaches roamed at will, and wherever they passed they left their mark, as Cochise had sworn, in the bones and the memories of his enemies.

As he rode along silently, lost in his thoughts, Jeffords heard his name called by Jed Hawkins, the boss of the wagon train. Hawkins rode up to him excitedly. "Looks like we might get some fresh game, Cap Jeffords. There it is again. Listen!"

What sounded like the call of a wild turkey came from about a quarter of a mile ahead.

"Nothing tastes so good as wild turkey," Hawkins said. "Want to get in on a little shooting, Cap?"

Jeffords cocked his ear and listened again. Then he said: "That's not wild turkey. That's Indian."

"Indian!" Hawkins roared. "I know the sound of turkey."

A rocky canyon cut down ahead of them. Jeffords searched it swiftly. "The Indians expect that you do, Mr. Hawkins. They can imitate turkey calls so expertly they fool the turkeys. They're trying to get us to separate in those rocks and brush. We're carrying breechloaders and they're afraid to come out into the open."

Hawkins, a farmer from Kansas, looked at Jeffords for a moment and then he laughed loudly again. "You Westerners have a sense of humor, Captain Jeffords. But we're not that green! I can tell gobbler when I hear it. I guess you folks out here try to play all us travelers for fools."

Shaking his head, Hawkins rode off.

"Hold it!" Jeffords said. Hawkins slowed up. He looked

puzzled and a little angry. Jeffords rode past him and then turned his horse to the right. "It's almost noon, Mr. Hawkins," Jeffords said. "Wild turkeys gobble on the roost. Never as late as this in the morning. If we had jumped turkey they'd be off in the brush, out of reach."

"A joke's a joke," Hawkins said peevishly.

"They want to draw a few men ahead of the rest of us. They'd have them shot and stripped and be away before anybody could stop them."

Hawkins spat. "You folks are always talking Indians!"

Jeffords lifted his rifle suddenly and fired. There was a scream of pain. An Indian leaped up. Two other Indians rose from behind rocks and scurried up the canyon. The wounded Indian raised his gun. Jeffords fired again. The Indian fell dead.

Hawkins was white. "Holy Moses!" he said. "Holy Moses!"

Jeffords rode up to the Indian. He held his revolver ready. Then he slipped the revolver into his holster. "He's dead," he said.

One of the other men dismounted and drew a knife. "What are you going to do?" Jeffords asked.

"Scalp me an Indian." The man grinned. "Fellow tells me you can weave their hair good for a saddle decoration."

"Forget it."

"He's dead, ain't he?"

"Forget it," Jeffords repeated. "Get back on your horse."

"You ain't the boss!" The man knelt before the Indian.

"Get back on your horse," Jeffords said softly.

The man turned and looked at Jeffords. For a moment he hesitated, the knife in his hand, and then he caught something in Jeffords's blue eyes and he got up slowly and walked back to his horse. "Every Westerner I ever met has scalped an Indian," he said.

"You're not a Westerner yet," Jeffords said.

"Do what he says and shut up," Hawkins said to the man. "I'm asking your pardon, Captain Jeffords. I guess we're all a little green."

A troop of mounted soldiers rode out to greet the wagon train when it arrived at the east entrance to Apache Pass. The lieutenant in command said the detachment was stationed at Fort Bowie and would give the train the military protection necessary for it to get through the pass in safety.

"Those Apaches raise the very devil with us," the lieutenant said. "You'd think they would keep away from a place like Fort Bowie — high walls, men on guard all the time. But they come right down to the walls and if we don't keep our eyes peeled they steal horses right out of our corrals! They've attacked travelers a hundred yards from the fort."

The wagon train stopped for water at the springs and Jeffords went off by himself and looked at the scars which were still on the sides of the hills from the howitzers fired by Captain Roberts's men.

The lieutenant joined him. He pointed to the fort. "First time you've seen it, sir?" he asked.

"Yes," Jeffords said.

[131]

"We needed this place here. They tell me there used to be fighting here all the time."

"I know," Jeffords said. He looked again at the pock-marked hills.

The soldiers remained with the pioneers until they were well out of the pass. Jeffords guided the train into the Santa Cruz Valley and then in the distance he made out the church and then some of the other buildings in Tucson. When they reached the Old Pueblo, they discovered the city was too crowded with other travelers for them to enter. Hawkins parked the wagons in a circle just outside the city walls, and then Jeffords bade him farewell and rode into Tucson alone.

The city was changed, he thought, as he rode slowly down a street packed with people. Not so much on the outside, but he could feel the difference. There were a few more stores, a few more saloons. The streets were still unpaved. But the place was more American now than it had been when he last was there. The Mexicans were giving way to their conquerors.

He went to a rooming house he remembered — a place called the Scat Fly, because the waiters in the dining room seemed to spend most of their time swinging at flies — and he engaged a room. He cleaned up and went down to the dining room. Some men were seated around a large table, and Jeffords recognized one of them as Silas St. John. He nodded pleasantly and said: "Hello, Mr. St. John."

St. John rose immediately and held out his hand. "Tom Jeffords! Welcome back to Tucson."

St. John introduced him to the other men at the table. One of them, Milton Duffield, caught Jeffords's eye. Duffield was an enormous man. He wore the sober black clothes of an Eastern businessman. His face was swarthy. As Jeffords shook his hand, he said, "Seems that I've heard of you before, Mr. Duffield. Didn't you come out here as marshal?"

"Right," Duffield said in a rumbling voice. "I resigned. I'm mail inspector now."

Place was made for Jeffords at the table and he sat down. "Mail?" he asked.

"Does that surprise you, Captain Jeffords?" Duffield asked. "Well, we do have mail — of sorts."

The meal was sumptuous. There was fried steak, and there were potatoes and several kinds of Mexican dishes. When Duffield finished, he stood up and said: "I'm mighty pleased to meet you, Captain Jeffords. Consider Milt Duffield your friend." Leaving a trail of smoke from a black cigar, Duffield strode across the room, slapping the backs of friends. At the door he picked up a black silk plug hat and clapped it on his head.

"Are they letting hats like that walk around Tucson now?" Jeffords asked.

"Nobody would take a shot at Milt Duffield," one of the other diners said.

"I guess he's the only man in the Territory of Arizona

who could get away with a silk topper," St. John laughed. "He's the handiest man around here with a gun. He likes to put the point of a ten-penny nail into an adobe wall — and then shoot the nail through the wall."

"Sounds like a good man to have on your side," Jeffords commented.

"I work for him," St. John said.

For several weeks Jeffords loafed around in Tucson and did nothing else. Various businessmen offered him jobs, but he turned them all down. He slept late and ate when he pleased. There was nothing in particular that he wanted to do.

But he was somehow not content. He also was a little bored. He had moved in danger during the war years and now it was difficult to slow down. One day he got together some gear and went prospecting in the hills. When he returned from the solitary journey he felt more calm and rested. He was more cheerful than he had been at any time since arriving in Tucson.

"That's marvelous country out there," he said to St. John. "It's like no place on earth — at least no place I've ever seen."

St. John nodded. "Yes," he said. "There could be a wonderful future for the Arizona Territory."

"Except for the Indians."

"Except for the Indians," St. John agreed.

"What are they doing about it, except sending out useless posses?" Jeffords asked.

"Worse than nothing. I had some hopes that when they made this a separate Territory that we might be able to get something done. But if anything, it's worse. The first thing the Governor did was proclaim the Indian the greatest menace to the future of Arizona. From that time on the Territorial Legislature has done nothing but ask Washington to send money and troops out here to wipe out the Apaches."

"Hasn't anybody tried to talk to the Indians?"

"Oh, some general came out here and went to Bowie and tried to get an interview with Cochise. Perhaps he was on the level. Only he was handicapped: the last five times the Americans tried to make a deal with Indians it somehow truned out that the Indians were shot or poisoned. Cochise wouldn't see him, and the general went off, more an Indian-hater than ever."

There was a commotion near the bar in the saloon where the two men were talking. They looked up. Duffield was showing off his great strength. He had taken off his long black coat and had rolled up a shirt sleeve. He took a heavy chair by one of its legs and held it at arm's length and then lifted it. The crowd around him cheered.

"Let's see you lift somebody," a man shouted.

"Try a gal!" another man yelled.

"A gal is too light," Duffield said. He looked around. "Hey, Jeffords, come over here!" When Jeffords did not move, he shouted again: "Did you hear me, Jeffords?"

"Better humor him, Tom," St. John said. "He turns mean when he's been drinking."

Duffield walked over to them. His face was flushed and his eyes looked dangerous. "I called you, Jeffords!"

"I heard you."

"People come when I call them."

Jeffords finished his drink. His fingers fell on his gun belt. "Do they?" he asked pleasantly.

The room quieted suddenly. Duffield looked down at Jeffords, who was sitting carelessly, his long legs stretched out. Duffield laughed loudly. "Folks want to see if I can lift a man by the ankles, Jeffords," he said. "Like to try?"

Jeffords smiled. His hand fell to his side. "Sure."

"If I don't, I'll buy you a drink."

"Sure." Jeffords stood up. Duffield squatted and seized his ankles. He started to lift. His face got red and the veins bulged on his forehead. The crowd came closer. Then Duffield bunched his powerful muscles and he lifted Jeffords six inches from the floor. He released him and stood up, panting. "Reckon I did it," he said.

"Reckon you did," Jeffords said. "Sit down and let me buy you a drink."

Duffield sat down, still breathing hard. His eyes, fixed on Jeffords, were clear and penetrating, and Jeffords had the sudden realization that Duffield was not at all drunk. "Here's to you, Captain Jeffords," Duffield said, raising his glass. He emptied the glass and set it on the table. "I'd like to see you tomorrow," he said.

"Any time."

"I need you, Captain Jeffords."

"Need me? For what?"

"The government needs you. The mail situation is terrible."

"What have I got to do with mail?"

"This is no place to talk. Will you come to my office tomorrow?"

"Sure."

Duffield fingered the glass. "I didn't fool you a while ago."

"No."

"I have my own way of trying to size up a man."

"I'll be around tomorrow," Jeffords said.

Duffield looked up. He was freshly shaved and his black suit was immaculate. He wore clean white linen.

"Sit down, Captain Jeffords. I'm mighty glad to see you this morning." He offered Jeffords a cheroot and lit it for him. "I told you last night I needed you bad. I say it again today. I got a real job for you to do. It ain't worth nothing in money — but it's a job that needs doing."

Jeffords puffed slowly. "Go on."

"The mail situation is plain lousy," Duffield said earnestly. "What with Indians and clerks who line their pockets and one thing and another — Tucson might as well be in the middle of the Pacific Ocean. The government can't hire riders. Too much risk. Mail takes months to get here — months to get out. There's no schedule. I got to keep on the move all the time to see that the clerks at one place or another don't run off with government funds." He leaned forward and put a large hand on Jeffords's knee. "How would you like the job of supervising mail between here and Fort Bowie?"

"I don't know anything about mail."

"Ain't nothing to know about mail. St. John knows about mail and he's doing as good a job as he can. But mail riders are worse than mules. He can't handle them. Nobody else in this damned town will take the job. Everybody is too busy trying to get rich and trying to kill Indians. Want the job?"

"Why me?" Jeffords asked.

Duffield sat back. He eyed Jeffords shrewdly. "I know men. You ain't about to go to work for some business firm here. I don't think you're thinking about going to work for one of the big mines. And you don't have the look of a rancher."

"Since I don't seem to be the kind of man to make a living in an ordinary way you think I'm fit to work for the government," Jeffords said dryly.

Duffield straightened with sudden pride. "I work for the government, Captain Jeffords! Somebody has to keep government business moving in a place like this. Do you want the job?"

Jeffords knocked the ash from his cheroot. "I'll try it," he said.

"Good!" Duffield boomed. "You're working, as of now!" He raised his head. "St. John!" When St. John entered the office, Duffield said: "Jeffords is going to work for us."

St. John smiled broadly. "Excellent!"

"St. John will show you how this office *doesn't* run,"

Duffield said. "You make it run! You understand, Captain Jeffords, when I say I want it run right, I'm speaking for the government. You now are working for the United States."

He picked up his black silk hat and left the office. Jeffords sighed. Then he looked at St. John and grinned. "Maybe you'd better tell me something about the mail business, Silas," he said.

St. John filled him in quickly. The big trouble, as Jeffords already surmised, was through the Apache country. The riders used the abandoned Butterfield stations as depots — but the country between the stations was deadly.

"The riders get paid a hundred and twenty-five dollars a month," St. John said.

"That's good pay."

"Few of them ever live to collect it," St. John said quietly.

CHAPTER XIII

Jeffords heard the clatter of hoofs and looked out of the window. He saw a military patrol from Fort Lowell, just outside of Tucson, and before he stepped outside the office to listen to the officer in command he knew why the men were there. The lieutenant leaned down from his saddle and handed him a leather mail pouch.

"Where did it happen this time?" Jeffords asked.

"About fifteen miles out," the officer said. "We found the rider's body. Or what was left of it."

"Burned?"

"To a crisp. Nothing left but bones. We found some of the mail scattered around — and this bag. Looks like they cut it open and then threw it away." The lieutenant shook his head. "Never found a bag thrown away before. Apaches like to keep them."

"Thanks," Jeffords said.

"Looks like old Cochise isn't fixing to let any mail go through," the lieutenant said. "Last rider, before you took on, was handled the same way." He laughed shortly. "I don't see why anybody would take that kind of job."

Jeffords returned to his office, the torn pouch in his hand. St. John looked up. "Another one?"

"Yes."

"That makes three out of the last four." St. John looked at the pouch curiously. "Odd that they didn't keep that. The Apaches use them to store dried meat."

Jeffords sat down. He bit off the end of a cigar and lit it thoughtfully. "I wonder if Cochise is saying hello to me — personally — in his own way."

"You might have something there," St. John agreed. "You can bet he knows that a new man has taken over here. Nobody has ever found out how he does it, but he seems to know what's going on almost before it happens."

Jeffords blew out a mouthful of smoke. He held up the bag. "Indians don't waste things. This is a gesture of contempt."

"Maybe Cochise is trying to show he has so many of those bags he doesn't need any more." St. John laughed grimly. "God knows, everybody in his tribe, down to the last little papoose, must own a government mailbag!"

Jeffords stuffed the recovered mail into a new pouch, already half filled with letters. Then he examined his revolver with great care. He took a carbine from the wall rack.

St. John watched him, frowning. "You're not going out yourself."

"I need a little air," Jeffords said. "Been cooped up too long."

St. John stood up. "That's not your job, Tom."

"There ought to be a rider from the East waiting at Bowie, oughtn't there?"

"If he got there alive."

"I'll swap pouches with him." He hefted the bag. "Not much in it to have a man killed for, is there?"

"Andy MacDowell is over at the Congress Hall," St. John said. "He's ready to go."

"He just got paid for last month, didn't he?"

"Yes."

"Then let him enjoy it. It isn't often a mail rider gets to spend the money he earns." He swung the pouch over his shoulder. "See you."

"I think you're crazy, Tom."

Jeffords paused at the door for a moment. "I don't like to order men to do something I don't do myself."

Jeffords reached the Bowie mail depot without encountering Indians. He exchanged pouches with the rider bringing the mail from the East, and, after a short rest, started back. He rode slowly, resting his horse frequently. He rode through the night. There was a full moon. The country was well lighted. The silver decorations on the saddle glinted in the pale light.

There was a faint reflection on the trail ahead of him and he turned and saw the dawn like a broad paint streak in the east. It was very quiet. There was no sound except the horse's hoofs and the crunch of leather under him. He breathed deeply. It was a good sound. It got brighter. The sky was stainless. He was a little tired. He was in the Santa Cruz Valley now and it would not be too long.

The valley lay long before him. He thought it was a beautiful sight. The air was sweet and fresh and the sun rose new here each day, each day a beginning, what happened yesterday gone and ended.

There were several large boulders ahead of him and before his mind translated their strangeness he automatically drew in his horse. Something flickered in him as he stared at the rocks, lying so naturally near the trail. Then he lifted his carbine and fired and one of the boulders let out a yell of pain and the rock became a gray blanket and the Indian under it rose and then fell.

Jeffords fired again and twisted on his horse, sliding down the side of the animal, riding so that the horse was between him and the Indians. He jabbed his spurs into the horse's side and he heard the whine of bullets over him. The Indians were on foot — and as far as he could see, there were no horses waiting near by.

He felt a pain in his side and another in his arm. He heard the low hum of arrows. There were three other Indians behind a clump of palo verdes. He fired again and broke his horse into a gallop again and then he was in the clear.

He felt a wetness on his right side. He saw the tail of an arrow sticking out of his jacket. Another arrow had cut through his arm. He held the reins in his teeth and pulled out the arrow from his side. His face broke out in sweat.

He opened his leather jacket. The wound in his side did not seem too deep. He jammed a kerchief against it and kept his elbow pressed against the kerchief. His arm was bleeding and the blood ran out over his fingers.

He wondered about poison. The Apaches used poison occasionally when they meant business. Cochise meant plenty of business. They used poisonous plants and mixed the poison with deer blood.

He ought to know pretty soon, he thought. With all the bouncing the horse was giving him, if there were any poison it ought to be all the way through him before long.

After a while he decided that maybe the arrows hadn't been poisoned. His right arm was stiff and it hurt and he felt sleepy but it was not the poison kind of feeling. He had to stay awake. He had to stay awake and in the saddle. He knew he wouldn't remain alive through the night if he didn't stay in the saddle.

Presently he could see Tucson. He was very glad to see it. He was getting very tired. He was swaying in the saddle. He knew that if he were attacked again now and he had to shoot he could not shoot very straight. He could taste the salt of his sweat. He was almost at the outskirts of the town now. Then he was inside the town. He was very sleepy. He rode up to the mail office. He tried to yell to St. John but he couldn't make it come out very loud. He slid slowly down the side of his horse. He fell to his knees. He felt someone pick him up and then he passed out.

When he opened his eyes it seemed a long time later. He

was sprawled in a chair in the office. St. John said: "Somebody went for the army doctor."

Before the doctor arrived, Jeffords passed out again. From a long distance he heard St. John ask: "Is it serious?"

He heard the doctor say: "He's built like a horse. He'll be all right."

Jeffords was up and around in a few days. People around town congratulated him on his close shave. He thanked them abstractedly. St. John, watching him, knew that he had something new on his mind.

The next rider got through. The one after that disappeared and never again was heard from. The one after that was shot, but managed to get through. The next two were killed.

Jeffords took to staying away from the mail office in the afternoons. St. John asked no questions. He knew that when Jeffords was ready to speak he would do so.

The riders continued to be attacked. Jeffords tried sending them out in pairs. That helped a little, but not much, and it ran over the budget the government allowed. By summer, six more riders were killed or wounded and two others were missing.

Then one day Jeffords called St. John into his office. "I'm going up to see Cochise," he said.

St. John was silent for a long time. "I thought you would, eventually," he said.

"You've been wondering where I've been going in the afternoons, the last few months," Jeffords said. "I've been studying how to speak Apache. I found an Apache boy at the San Xavier Mission. He told me yesterday I knew enough to be able to talk to Cochise."

"You are going at this the right way," St. John said with great earnestness.

"Not only the language," Jeffords continued. "But the customs and the manners and the traditions — everything. I've learned a lot." He looked at his cigar. "They're quite a people — the Apaches." Then he said: "The boy told me that Cochise is camped in the Graham Mountains. He said he would take me part of the way."

"Can you trust the boy?"

"I don't know. I believe so. He's proud of his people. It wasn't too hard for me to make him understand after a while that I agreed with him." He nodded slowly. "They're some people."

"You know that for five years now no white man has seen Cochise and lived," St. John said quietly.

"I thought about all that. But somebody's got to get to him and get things straightened out. People can't go around killing each other forever. I think maybe Cochise is human." His chin rose. "I'll gamble on that."

St. John nodded slowly. "I think I somehow always thought you and Cochise would get together some day. From the beginning, from when I met him — right after I met you."

"Tell me what you remember about him."

St. John leaned back. "It's curious, Tom, but I've never been able to square away my memory of Cochise with the man who's been fighting this bloody war. I have always thought of him as a man of peace — a man of honor. I probably could get lynched in Tucson if anybody else heard me say that. But if he gives you his word on anything — I think you could depend on it." Then he said: "You know there is a big chance that you won't get as far as seeing Cochise?"

"I know that," Jeffords said.

"And if they do let you stay alive long enough to face him personally — there isn't much chance that you'll leave that camp alive."

"I know that too," Jeffords said.

CHAPTER XIV

Cochise's camp in the Graham Mountains was about eighty miles to the north and east of Tucson. The Apache boy rode with Jeffords as far as the San Pedro River.

"I will not go beyond here," the boy, Juan, said. "Apaches who make peace with the white man are not loved by Cochise. If I were taken by him it would go worse with me than with you, maybe."

"You have done a good thing," Jeffords said, embracing the boy. "If there is any success in this, much of it will be because of your help."

"I wish you luck, Nantan Jeffords," Juan said. "It is said Cochise is the cruelest of our race. And yet it also is said there is nothing he admires more than a brave man." The youth raised his right arm gravely, and then he galloped away.

Jeffords dismounted. He looked around. It was quiet. He could see no living thing and yet he knew that he was being watched. He knew that keen eyes had picked him up before he was very long out of Tucson, and he knew that every foot of his journey was being constantly observed.

It was time now to set to work on the first part of the plan he had conceived to keep himself alive at least until he could face Cochise. He untied a small bundle of evergreen branches he had gathered while crossing the mountains. He built a small fire and placed some of the evergreen wood on the flames. He spread a blanket over the fire and then suddenly raised the blanket so that a black cloud of smoke columned upward. He covered the fire again and after a moment lifted it and permitted another shaft of smoke to rise in the still air. He waited five minutes and then repeated the performance.

He knew his smoke signal could be read for many miles. In smoke language, he was announcing that he was traveling alone and that his mission was one of peace. To reach Cochise without being cut down by Apache bullets, he had decided he had to arouse Indian curiosity, and he had decided that the best way to do that was to send ahead his own signals. He knew that no white men announced their intentions to Indians, and he hoped that they would be surprised enough to leave him alone.

He decided also that he would travel openly. He would make no attempt to hide or cover his tracks.

He put out the fire and rode off. He scanned the sky. He could see no other smoke signal. So far, he thought, it is going well.

He rode steadily through the afternoon. He reached the foothills of the Saddle Mountains and skirted to the south of them until he entered upon a flat land. In the distance he could make out the Graham peaks. He climbed down from the horse and built another fire and sent out another smoke signal.

He was deep in Indian country now. He continued slowly, casually, showing no concern, and then he came to the low approaches to the Grahams. The sun baked the hard, rocky earth and the terrible heat came from everywhere. The country was filled with boulders and he knew that behind many of the huge rocks were Apache Indians and that their fingers, even now, must be resting lightly on triggers, or clutching tightly the feathered tails of their arrows.

He climbed down again from his horse. His skin tingled. He made another fire and sent up another signal. This was nothing but a gesture. He knew that there were eyes on him from all directions and that there no longer was need to say where he was planning to go. He moved calmly, with deliberation. He must not make a false move. He must do nothing to excite his watchers. He needed only to make a single young Apache fighting man nervous — and it would be all over.

There was the quiet of the grave. He mounted his horse and rode again, slowly, erectly, his rifle plainly sheathed in its saddle scabbard, his elbows high, his hands plainly on the reins. Thus far the bluff had not been called, he thought. He had to keep on, exactly as he was doing, even though his blood raced through his body and his heart pounded.

There was no sound except for the ring of the horse's hoofs on the metallic earth. Then the horse whinnied nervously. He touched the horse's neck to calm it. He kept his eyes straight ahead and he felt that invisible doors were closing behind him. He had a sudden desire to wheel around and race off — and he knew he would not get ten yards before being riddled.

He rode straight up a narrow wash and then the gully turned sharply to the right. He followed it, and he was in the camp of the Apaches — and they were on all sides of him.

They had appeared noiselessly as though they had formed themselves out of the air. They looked at him without curiosity. Their silence was louder than any noise.

He moved to the center of the camp and got off the horse. A woman walked up to him. Her face was as blank as the other faces — and yet he felt she was trying to say something to him. He handed her the reins. She took them silently. He unbuckled his revolver belt and handed it to her. He pulled his knife from his sheath and gave that to her. Then, in a calm voice, he said, in perfect Apache: "Hold these things for me. I will need them when I leave."

A tall Indian, naked except for loincloth, his broad chest marked with the symbols of Holos, the Sun, and of Lightning, walked up to Jeffords. He said: "What makes you believe you will leave here alive?"

The Indian spoke in Spanish. He looked Jeffords full in the face and Jeffords knew he was Cochise.

Jeffords felt a calm come over him. He returned the gaze tranquilly. Then he said: "It is known that the chief of the Chiricahua Apaches is the greatest Indian leader. It is known that he respects bravery as he respects truth."

There was not a flicker in Cochise's eyes. After a prolonged silence during which it seemed to Jeffords that every Indian in the camp held his breath, Cochise said: "You are a brave man. I will listen to you."

Cochise walked to his wickiup and entered. Jeffords followed him in. A small black-and-white dog, hardly more than a puppy, ran up to Cochise and barked happily. Cochise scratched him on the ear and then the Indian leader sat down on his haunches. Jeffords sat down facing him.

The woman who had taken his horse and gear now appeared with two clay platters bearing food. Without speaking, Cochise began to eat, picking up chunks of meat with his fingers. Jeffords did the same. He discovered he was hungry and that the meat was excellent.

When they finished eating, Cochise said: "Speak."

"I am the boss of the white man's mail," Jeffords said. "Mail is signaling that white men use. Things are told on pieces of paper and when someone else receives the paper he can understand what is being said to him. It is the same as a smoke signal. This mail is carried by messengers. They have no interest in the mail. They do not know what is in the mail. They are poor men and they make their living carrying the signals back and forth."

He paused. Cochise remained silent.

"These men do not look for trouble," Jeffords continued. He felt sweat on his neck. He wondered whether Cochise was listening to him, or understanding him. He wondered whether his Apache was plain, so that his words were saying what he wanted them to say. He wet his dry lips. "These men do not make trouble. They are like the air which carries the smoke signals of the Apaches. Yet these men have been killed again and again by the Chiricahua warriors. I come to you to ask that these mail riders be permitted to travel in safety."

He paused again. Cochise remained motionless, his head bowed.

Jeffords's back was wet with sweat. "I come alone," he said. "I come without presents. I come only with a straight tongue to ask the Chiricahua chief to stop killing these men."

Cochise looked up suddenly. His black eyes were hard. "These men carry signals in the war against the Apaches!"

Jeffords shook his head. "No, such signals are carried by the military in other ways. I know, because I myself carried such messages for the military."

Cochise's eyes widened slightly. "You say this of yourself — to me?"

"I do not hide anything," Jeffords replied. "I have come to you to speak as a man speaks to another man. During the great war between white men I carried signals for the military. But the messages now carried by the men who work for me are messages of peace, between white men and their brothers in distant places. The messages do not work against the Indians."

Cochise was long in replying. The black eyes looked at Jeffords from across a long distance. This difference, Jeffords thought, was the space between the two of them, the space that had to be crossed.

"You are a brave man," Cochise said. "You speak with a straight tongue, maybe."

"There is no fork in my tongue. I have come to you without knowing whether I would live to return to my people. The end of my time may be now — or tomorrow. I have never spoken with a double tongue and I do not begin now."

Cochise's face lost some of its granite-like quality. He leaned forward. "Why should I do anything to help the white man?" His voice was more human and Jeffords felt a sudden feeling of hope. "For many harvests I was friend to the white man. I protected them against bad Indians. For my actions I was paid in treachery! For the lives I spared I was paid in death!"

He spoke rapidly, so that Jeffords was hard put to follow him. He told story after story of the betrayal of Indians by the white man. When he finished, Jeffords replied: "You do not tell the whole story. There are other stories. You are just and right in your hatred."

"Yet you come to me and ask me to spare the lives of these white men."

"I ask you to spare the lives of men who have caused you no injury."

"There are Indians who have caused your people no injury," Cochise retorted fiercely. "And yet they are hunted like animals and are killed. Do the white men try to find out which Indians are good and which are bad?"

"No."

"You ask me to be better than the white men?"

"I ask you to be greater than the white men," Jeffords said quietly.

Cochise stared at him in amazement. "You are a strange man and you ask strange favors."

"A man can give favors only according to his size," Jeffords said in the same quiet voice.

Cochise stood up abruptly and walked out of the wickiup. Jeffords went out after him. They stood on the edge of a rock overlooking the valley below. "It is quiet here," Cochise said.

"Yes."

"It is a good place."

"Yes."

"This is the country of the Apache. The Americans think they are better than other men. They make their own laws and they say these laws must be obeyed — even in a country that does not belong to them. Why?"

"You ask nothing I have not myself asked before," Jeffords said.

"I know your face! We have fought against each other!" Cochise said suddenly.

"I fought in the battle of Apache Pass before the fort was built," Jeffords said calmly.

"That day the fire-wagons were used!" Cochise said. "I remember that red beard. You were not a soldier. We would have won that fight until you turned the fire-wagons on us."

"I directed the use of the gun on wheels," Jeffords said.

Cochise touched Jeffords's shoulder. His face was serene. "Tagliato," he said, using the Apache word for "red beard," "I respect you."

"As I respect you, Cochise," Jeffords replied.

"Tagliato, we are friends."

"Yes."

"I will grant your request."

"Yes."

"We do not lie to each other."

"It will be a strange friendship," Jeffords said. "My people will not understand and your people will not understand."

"I do not speak of people," Cochise said, his voice hardening. "And you are not the same as your people."

"I do not believe I am, Cochise."

"We will speak the truth always and we will talk often and our talk will have in it nothing of anything else we may do. Your life is safe among my people, always."

"I cannot promise you the same, Cochise."

"I am the leader of the Chiricahua Apaches!"

Jeffords gripped Cochise's arm. "There will be a day when you will be able to walk among my people in safety."

"There is no value in many persons," Cochise said in a very low voice. "Through his life, a man is lucky if he finds a friend."

[156]

CHAPTER XV

Jeffords walked into the mail office. St. John leaped to his feet. "He let you return! Alive!"

Jeffords sat down wearily. "He promised to let the mail riders go through."

"Tom!"

"What's been happening since I left?"

"Nothing good," St. John said. "Apaches attacked a wagon train about forty miles east of here and killed everybody in it. Another band attacked a ranch in the Sonoita Valley and killed three men there."

"Anything else?"

"Some cattle were stolen, almost outside Tucson, and three soldiers were killed in a running fight."

Jeffords closed his eyes. He thought of Cochise and of the peace in his camp. "Have you got a load of mail ready to send out?"

"Yes," St. John said.

Jeffords rubbed his chin slowly. "Let it go," he said.

He left the office early. He went to the Congress Hall saloon. As soon as he entered, tongues began to buzz. The bartender looked at him curiously as he pushed a bottle and a small glass toward him. Jeffords poured himself a drink and lifted the glass to his lips. A great clap on the shoulder almost made him choke.

"Tom Jeffords!" Duffield bellowed. "I'm the happiest man in this lousy town to see you back. I want to buy you a drink and tell you that you got more guts than a rattler's got rattles!"

Jeffords wiped the spilled drink from his shirt.

"By God, any man who'll go alone to the camp of old Cochise is a man in my language and anybody who says different has got Milt Duffield to answer to!"

One of the men at the bar said: "Nobody's saying different, Milt."

Other men clustered around Jeffords, all asking questions at the same time.

"What happened, Cap?"

"What was it like?"

"Old Cochise try to grab your scalp?"

Duffield ordered silence in a voice that must have echoed

against the mountains. "Seems like everybody is doing the asking and nobody is giving this man a chance to do some answering. Now I say everybody close up and let the man speak!"

There was instant silence. Jeffords shifted uneasily. He poured another drink and finished it quickly. "There's not much to tell."

"You saw old Cochise?" Duffield demanded.

"Yes."

"What did he tell you?"

"The mail riders no longer will be attacked."

The voices rose excitedly. Even Duffield's shouting could not quiet the men. Then a deep voice boomed: "So the cutthroat promised he would let the mail riders live?"

Jeffords looked into the face of William Oury, one of the most prominent citizens of Tucson.

"That's what he said, Oury," Jeffords said.

"I want to listen some more."

"This is a public place."

"So Cochise is going to make an exception for your riders?"

"Seems to me I said that," Jeffords said.

"Do you believe him?"

Jeffords nodded. "Yes."

"Folks say you know Indians," Oury said sarcastically. "Did you ever know an Indian to keep his word?"

"No one you would ever know," Jeffords said evenly.

"Would you like to back up the great faith you have in this lying murderer?"

"Sure, Will."

"Say a hundred dollars?"

"You have a bet."

"Of course, you might be lucky. Cochise misses a couple, now and then."

Jeffords took a cigar from his pocket. "Since I have been running the mails there haven't been three riders in a row to get through." He lit the cigar. "The bet is that five men will leave here and five will arrive here without trouble from the Indians."

Oury nodded, his eyes gleaming. "You got a bet, mister."

"Wait a minute," Duffield protested. "Even if Cochise keeps his own galoots in line — there are other Indians around who don't like white men."

Oury laughed shortly. "Want to call it off, Jeffords?"

Jeffords looked at him. "The bet stands." He left the saloon.

The first rider reached Mesilla and the West-bound rider reached Tucson with a report of complete quiet in Apache country. Jeffords sent out the next man. He too was not molested and the second West-bound rider arrived in Tucson safely.

During the next few weeks the Apache attacks on other American parties continued unabated. Troops reported that Cochise's men had raided wagon trains, ranches, travelers, everywhere. A scouting party of thirty soldiers was attacked by a band of Indians led by Cochise himself. But the mail riders remained untouched.

Jeffords discovered he had become a celebrity in Tucson. The arrival of each mail rider was hailed. Many side-bets were made of the same nature as his wager with Oury. The mail office began to become the town hangout. Ranchers came in from miles away to await the outcome of the bet.

On the day the last rider was scheduled to come in a great crowd gathered in front of the mail office. By now Jeffords was ashamed of having made the bet. He felt as though he had in some way traded on Cochise's honor. The men, some of them drunk, lounged around the front of the office. It was late in the afternoon when someone shouted he saw dust in the distance; and then, a little later, the fifth and last rider galloped into Tucson.

Duffield, who had appointed himself referee, yelled: "Any trouble on the road?"

The rider slid down from his horse. "Quiet as a Sunday in the park," he grinned.

"No Indians?"

"Nary a sign."

Duffield raised his huge arms. "If nobody has got no objections, I will just announce that the contest is ended and that Cochise has kept his word. Gentlemen, pay your bets." He opened the door to the mail office. Jeffords was seated inside, smoking quietly. "Tom!" Duffield bellowed.

Jeffords got up and went outside. He looked at the rider and then at the men gathered.

"Looks like you won some money, son," Duffield said. "Here's your fifth man, safe and sound."

Oury walked up. He handed Jeffords a small bag of gold.

"I guess you still know your Indians, Jeffords," he said.

"What do you mean by that?"

"You won your bet, didn't you? That makes you know Indians better than I do."

Jeffords took the bag and tossed it to Duffield. "The priest needs some cash," he said. He walked back into the office.

"Now there is a great man," Duffield said admiringly. "Think of all the whisky this would buy!"

CHAPTER XVI

Tahzay, son of Cochise, was waiting for him when Tom Jeffords reached the narrow corridor leading up to the Stronghold, and Jeffords knew that it was a great honor.

Tahzay pointed to the Stronghold. "That is our home," he said proudly.

"There are two Strongholds, are there not?" Jeffords asked.

"Yes. The East Stronghold is very big. The West Stronghold is small but it is better to fight from."

As he rode alongside him toward the entrance to the Stronghold, Jeffords studied the son of Cochise. At twenty Tahzay was tall and strong. His face was quiet and thoughtful. He did not have the dynamic quality of his father, Jeffords thought. Perhaps he never would have it. Perhaps nature arranged things that way.

When it would be time for Tahzay to become the chief of the Chiricahua people, then perhaps it would be the time for a Tahzay and not for a Cochise. The fires were being put out, one after the other, Jeffords thought, and Tahzay was perhaps a step closer to what Apache Indians had to be if they were to survive in the white man's world.

On the way up the steep slope on the north side of the Stronghold, Jeffords felt himself relax. He felt he was passing not only into another world — but into another time as well. Tahzay turned to him and smiled. It was a pale, quiet smile that gave light to his face. He too was conscious of the honor of having been sent by his father to escort the white man to the rancheria.

As he entered the camp, however, Jeffords had a sudden change of feeling. He looked at the unhurried, quiet men who moved calmly among the wickiups and he realized these men were killers. Among them were men kin to Apaches he himself had killed. Who among them, he thought, had been on the last raid on the wagon train? Who had attacked the ranch near Tucson? Which man, now occupied so peacefully, had fired the shot which killed a soldier — a rancher — a pioneer?

Cochise stepped out of his wickiup. His face brightened

when he saw Jeffords. He embraced him when he dismounted. And then he stepped back and looked keenly at Jeffords. "You feel that you are a traitor to your people, Tagliato," he said slowly. "You feel that it is not good to come into the camp of the enemies of your white brothers."

"Your eyes see deeply, Cochise," Jeffords said.

"Your face was not meant to hide your feelings."

"I felt a cleanness and a peace in me until I entered the rancheria."

"And then you felt that you should be killing Apaches instead of walking among them as friend," Cochise said.

"May a man put himself apart from his own?" Jeffords asked bitterly.

Without answering, Cochise walked away. Jeffords followed him. The Indian leader took a twisting path which led upward until the two men were high on one of the walls of the Stronghold. Cochise climbed onto a huge rock. When Jeffords clambered up to his side, the rancheria lay below them. On all sides were the overpowering rocks.

"How long do you think these rocks have stood here, Tagliato?" Cochise asked.

"From the beginning."

"They make a world. They are filled with many things which live. There are trees that you can see. There are birds in the trees. Listen, Tagliato, you can hear the birds. There are rabbits. There are squirrels. There are insects and worms. There are snakes. And there are men and women. All these living things have a time on earth and then they are gone."

Cochise looked around slowly. His face was austere.

"To each living thing his own time is a lifetime," Cochise went on. "Things are measured by this lifetime. To the insect one or two days are long times. To the bird, his time is longer. To the bird the life of an insect must be very short. And so it is. To men and women all these things have a short life. How is it then to the rocks, Tagliato?"

He faced Jeffords and raised his long arms.

"The rocks have looked upon many men and women and have seen them live and die as we have seen dogs live and die. The rocks must think often that the reason for all these things is unimportant. The life of a man must be less to them than the life of a flea is to us." Cochise's dark eyes glowed. "You have asked me whether a man may step apart from his own people — whether a friendship may live between two men whose people war against each other. The answer is a double one and it is no answer, maybe. The answer is that it is possible and that it is not possible. It is possible because nothing that passes between people is important. Lift your eyes, Tagliato! Look around you. We are lost in time and we are lost in space and we are very small! What we do is of as much importance as what two ants arrange to do! How many men have sat here where we sit now — and what is left of them and the things they arranged?

"And yet the other answer is right too. Because a man is the limit of his kind. He can go no farther than his own manhood. It is only in knowing — in exchanging ideas — in counseling and receiving counsel — that a man may step

[166]

beyond himself and gain the wisdom and strength of two men. A man moves toward his death each day, and the death is the final part of his life — the most important part, maybe — but with a friend at his side, he moves with two hearts."

Now his voice took on fire. Jeffords felt small and very young.

"There is nothing that we do ourselves, Tagliato. Each man is driven. Each man is like an arrow. The string is pulled back, and the arrow goes in the direction it is pointed — and although it seems to have life it has no life. Soon it falls to the ground, and is again a piece of wood. Your people and my people kill each other, Tagliato. One day we will try to kill each other maybe." A faint smile appeared on his lips. "If I die of a bullet I hope that it is your bullet. The life of a man is a precious thing. It is better to give that life to a friend — than to an enemy."

"You have given me answer," Jeffords said.

"It is good to ask questions. I am tired of what goes on inside my head. It is like a country I have seen too often. Now I have your head to look into. And you have mine. We must look into each other as though each of us were an unexplored land — filled with many new things. If we speak with straight tongues your mind will be as though it were mine, and mine as though it were yours."

"Do you believe that the minds of other men may one day do the same?" Jeffords asked.

Cochise's manner changed abruptly. "I do not speak for other men," he said harshly.

After the evening meal the people gathered around the fire. Jeffords tried to pick out the faces he remembered from the other time. His eyes met Nahilzay's and he felt a flicker of warning. There was danger there, he thought. Then Jeffords met Chee, a son of Mangas Coloradas, who was being brought up by Cochise.

A tall, lanky, incredibly ugly Indian named Teese, who was a kind of court jester to Cochise, walked up to Jeffords and then reared back as though the sight of the white man blinded him. He put his hands in front of his eyes, as though he were shading them from the sun. Then, while the Indians laughed heartily, he sprang back and forth, pretending to work up courage. Finally he came close to Jeffords, and touched his red beard gingerly. He jerked his fingers back as though they had been burned. The Indians roared. The pantomime was funny and Jeffords laughed as loudly as the rest. Then Jeffords picked up a gourd of water and with a sympathetic expression on his face, poured the water on the Indian's fingers. The Indians shouted their approval.

Tahzay handed his father an earthenware jug. Cochise offered the jug to Jeffords. Jeffords drank from it and then he felt sick. "What is this?"

"Castor oil," Cochise said with satisfaction. He took the jug and drank deeply from it. He nodded with pleasure. "This is good for the stomach," he said.

Jeffords watched the jug pass from man to man. "There are some things in which we will always be different," he said to Cochise. "Among us, castor oil is for ailing children."

After a while Cochise said: "Do you know about the coyote stories, Tagliato? Now you will hear some of them. Coyote is a great figure. He has a nature everybody understands. He is good at tricking other animals — and people too. And he often gets tricked himself."

Pionsenay told the first story. "Coyote tried to catch a turkey one day," he said. "Turkey was up a tree. Coyote tried to catch Turkey by chopping down the tree. Just as the tree was going to fall, Turkey flew to another tree. Coyote chopped down the tree. Turkey flew to another tree. Finally Coyote was tired. He collapsed and Turkey got away."

The men nodded gravely. Nahilzay spoke. As he uttered the first words, Jeffords knew the story would in some way apply to him. "Coyote met Bumblebee one day," Nahilzay said. "Bumblebee had something in his hand. Coyote asked him: 'What do you have there, old man?' Bumblebee said: 'I don't want anybody to meddle with this.' Coyote pleaded, but Bumblebee said: 'This is not for you.' But Coyote insisted and finally Bumblebee said: 'All right, but you cannot see it here. You must take it home and take it inside your hut and close the door so nothing can get inside or out. Then open the package.' Coyote grabbed the package and raced home and did as he was told and he opened the package and inside there were many bumblebees and they started to sting him. He screamed for help but the bumblebees stung him to death."

During the recital, Nahilzay looked steadily at Jeffords. Cochise's eyes were thoughtful.

"Coyote met a quail," Tahzay said in his pleasant voice. "Quail had all his family lined up in a straight row behind him. Coyote asked him: 'How did you ever get them in such a straight line?' Quail said: 'I will tell you. This is what I did. I sharpened a stick and then I took a long rope and I lined up my family. The mother was at the head and the children were behind her. Then I pushed a stick through all their hearts and pulled the rope through it. They walked that way for a while and then I took the rope out and now they walk in a straight line.' Coyote raced home and told his wife about it and ordered her to line up the family. Then he sharpened a stick and got a long rope and he pierced the heart of his wife and after that the hearts of all his children and he drew the rope through the holes he had made. When he was through he noticed his family was lying down. He said: 'Hey, it's not time to sleep yet. Get up!' But when he looked closer he found they were dead."

Now Teese raised his hand. "Coyote had some money — just a little bit — and he was walking along, trying to think how he could change that money into something more valuable. Then he saw some American prospectors . . ."

Cochise turned to Jeffords and grinned.

"They had horses and mules and provisions and blankets and guns and plenty of ammunition," Teese went on. "Coyote had a brilliant thought. He put his money into the branches of a tree. When the Americans rode up they asked him what he was doing. 'I am watching this tree, it is very valuable,' Coyote said. 'Money grows on this tree.' The prospectors laughed at him so Coyote shook the tree a little and some of the money fell out. Now the men were interested. 'Sell us the tree,' they said. 'No,' Coyote said, pretending not to want to. 'This is the only tree in the world that grows money.' The prospectors said: 'We will give you everything we have. Our horses and mules and everything else. We will just climb down and you can have everything.' Coyote pretended not to want to and then he let the prospectors persuade him. 'All right,' he said finally. 'I will sell you the tree. There is only one thing. See those blue mountains over there? Well, you will have to wait until I get there. If you shake the tree before that nothing will come out and you will spoil it forever.' The prospectors agreed and Coyote jumped on one of the horses and rode away with everything. When he reached the mountains the men shook the tree. Only one piece of money fell out. That was the last of the money Coyote had put into the tree!"

The men continued to tell the old stories as the moon crept across the Stronghold. It was Nahilzay who told the final story.

"Coyote found some rabbits playing with their eyes under a high cliff," he said. "The rabbits tossed their eyes high into the air and the eyes fell down and fell into their places again. 'That is a wonderful game,' Coyote said. 'Let me play it.' The rabbits said: 'Go away, you might lose your eyes.' But Coyote insisted and the rabbits took his eyes and threw them into the air and they fell back into their places. 'That is enough for you,' they said. 'Now go away.' But Coyote insisted: 'Let me play just once more.' So they threw his eyes up again and while the eyes were up in the air one of the rabbits said: 'Let the eyes stick to something and never come back.' And the eyes did not come back and from then on Coyote was blind."

As the men walked away from the fire, Cochise said: "I have had a wickiup built for you, Tagliato. It is not far from my own."

"Nahilzay wants to be an enemy," Jeffords said.

"You have no enemies in this camp," Cochise said.

The next day a rider came into the camp with the report that a large herd of deer was grazing toward the north end of the Sulphur Spring Valley — a rare thing now — and the Indians organized a hunt immediately. The men went to their wickiups to get their weapons. Cochise asked Jeffords if he would like to go along. Jeffords agreed willingly. "I will get my gun," he said.

Cochise shook his head. "No gun. Only arrows. Guns make too much noise. If we used guns there would be no animals at all."

Jeffords laughed. "I never shot an arrow in my life."

"I will give you a bow and some arrows," Cochise said. "You can start to learn now."

When Cochise gave him a bow and a quiver filled with arrows, Jeffords looked at them dubiously. "I could not hit the side of a mountain with these."

"Try a few shots," Cochise said.

Jeffords fitted an arrow clumsily to the bow and then he looked around for something to shoot at. A few Indians gathered around to watch him. Teese, with a grimace, fastened a piece of red flannel to a tree. Jeffords aimed carefully. The arrow sped far to the left of the tree. The Indians slapped their thighs in glee and Jeffords grinned. He tried again. The arrow went even farther away from the target.

A sarcastic voice said: "Perhaps the white man should stand no farther than the length of an arm away from the target."

Jeffords whirled. Nahilzay was regarding him with amused contempt. Jeffords tightened his lips and tried again. With his fourth arrow he managed to hit the tree. He tried to make a joke of it. "I will go to the hunt, Cochise," he said, "but only for the ride."

Nahilzay stepped up to where Jeffords had stood. Then, so swiftly that the movement of his arm could scarcely be seen, he reached over his shoulder and took an arrow from the quiver, fitted it to the bow, loosed it, and before the arrow had struck dead into the center of the red flannel, he had a second arrow on the way and then a third and a fourth and a fifth. There was no break in his actions and when he was finished there were five arrows pinning the red flannel to the tree.

The women cried: "Yieaaaah! Yieaaaah!" The men nodded their heads gravely and then they all looked at Jeffords, and the white man read an important question in their eyes.

There was a queer tension in the air. Jeffords understood that it had worked out so that he was on trial. What had started out to be funny — his clumsy, inexperienced attempts to shoot arrows — had been challenged, in a serious way, by Nahilzay. The next move was up to him. Even Cochise made no move.

Jeffords went to his wickiup. He buckled on his cartridge belt. He returned to the Indians. He took a silver dollar from his pocket and rubbed it on both sides against his pants until the silver shone. He tossed it into the air once or twice and the sunlight reflected brightly on it. Then he flipped it into the air again and almost with the same movement pulled his revolver from its holster and fired and the coin rang silverly and when it fell to the ground Tahzay picked it up. It was twisted out of shape. Tahzay gave it to Jeffords. Jeffords tossed it to Nahilzay, who caught it automatically — and then threw it to the ground.

Teese ran over to Jeffords and hugged him. Jeffords offered him a cigar. He lit it for him. "Now walk to the tree," Jeffords said. Teese puffed out a mouthful of smoke and looked at Jeffords puzzled. "As a favor to me," Jeffords said. Teese walked to the tree. "Turn sideways and leave the cigar in your mouth," Jeffords said.

Now Teese understood and he put out his long arms in protest and contorted his face painfully around the cigar. Then he stopped clowning. He stood so his profile was toward Jeffords and the long cigar stuck out of his face and then Jeffords dropped his hand to the butt of his gun and without taking the weapon from the holster he fired and the cigar was clipped in the middle and fell away, leaving a small stump in Teese's mouth.

The women screamed and slapped their hands together.

Jeffords picked up the bow and quiver and walked to Nahil-zay. "Maybe you will teach me how to use this," Jeffords said.

Nahilzay's eyes shot with hatred. "Each man to his own weapon, white man!"

Jeffords picked up the twisted silver dollar. "Would you like to keep this?" he asked quietly. "To make your memory stay fresh?"

The hunters crossed Sulphur Spring Valley. At a signal from Cochise they broke into two bands. The first band, led by Cochise, rode about a quarter of a mile in front of the second band, led by Tahzay.

The riders spread out so that each rider was about fifty yards from the rider on either side of him. The two lines of hunters continued their advance until the herd of deer was sighted about half a mile ahead of them.

"Now watch!" Cochise said to Jeffords.

The first line of men raced ahead, the ends moving faster than the center, making the straight line into a huge U. Then the men swept around the deer in a great circle, the two ends coming together finally.

The second line of riders made a circle around the first circle, so that the deer were now surrounded by two rings of hunters, one inside the other. Until then the Indians had ridden in silence but when the outer circle was closed they began to yell. The deer milled around in panic.

The riders closed in on the deer, the spaces between the men growing less and less. No animal could pass out of the inner ring without coming within range of a rider, and if the animal succeeded in getting through the first ring, he then had to go through the second.

The Indians fired arrow after arrow. The animals tumbled over by the score. Jeffords, caught in the excitement, succeeded in hitting two deer. When the hunt was over there were more than a hundred dead animals on the grassy floor of the valley.

Cochise left a dozen warriors to get the animals together and the other hunters started back for the Stronghold, singing lustily. Cleaning the animals and bringing them to camp was woman's work. There would be plenty of fresh meat for some time to come.

Tahzay told Jeffords a story illustrating the hunting etiquette of the Apaches. When an Apache killed an animal and a less successful hunter came up to him the fortunate hunter was required to offer his kill to the other man, asking only: "What you don't need, leave for me."

Since the hide was the most important part of the animal, usually, the man who made the kill had to allow the other man to take it if he wanted it. The courtesy was followed so rigidly that a man who killed an animal in the company of other men was said, in the Apache phrase, to "kill it for his friend."

Now two men were out hunting together, Tahzay said. Both were excellent shots. They came upon a big deer — so close that neither could have missed it if he tried. "Each of these men tried to make the other one shoot the deer so he could have the skin," Tahzay said. "They made many excuses. One man said: 'I have shot many for you. You kill this deer. I need the hide.' While they were arguing the deer ran away and neither of them got it."

Jeffords laughed. Cochise nodded approvingly to his son, and Tahzay tried not to show the happiness he still felt when he said or did anything that pleased Cochise.

"How did you like the hunt?" Cochise asked Jeffords.

"It was good."

"One day I will show you how we use deer masks."

"Deer masks?"

"We will join the deer. Ho! They are surprised when they find that two of the 'deer' among them are men!"

Jeffords showed his amazement in his face. "Do you mean you mingle with the deer?"

"You will see, Tagliato. There are many things I will show you."

"I believe you," Jeffords said with vast sincerity.

"I will teach you how to use the bow and arrow. You need no teaching from me in the use of your own weapons." That was the first reference Cochise had made to the incident with Nahilzay.

The women hastened out with pack mules and several hours later began to return with the game. Jeffords watched with great interest as Tesalbestinay set to work skinning one of the animals. She cut away meat which would be eaten immediately, and then prepared the rest for drying. She cut the thick parts into thin strips and hung them in the sun.

When they were dried she pounded them with stones and when the strips were soft and very thin she buried them in a cool place.

She discarded the heart, because the Apaches believed it bad to eat the heart. Then she took the brains and put them to one side. She scraped off the remaining flesh on the skin with a sharpened deer bone and put the skins in a basin made from a stiffened hide.

She took a skin which was stretched out on the ground and put it in another leather basin. She poured hot water on it and then put in the brains from the deer. She worked the skin in the solution until it was soft. When it felt right to her she took it out and let it dry for a little while and then she began to stretch it, holding one end on the ground with her foot.

Jeffords offered to help her. She refused with a smile. "Occupy yourself with something else, Tagliato," she said. "Take the bow and arrow and practice. Maybe in a little while you will be good enough to go out with boys as a novice."

Jeffords laughed and tugged his beard. The wife of Cochise laughed with him. Then she stopped. "Be careful," she said. "Arrows make no sound." She walked over to him. "You have made a change here," she said seriously. "I have given thanks for it. My husband is a different man since you came here. For a long time he had the ghost sickness. Sometimes I thought it would break out of his head. He has no thoughts that I do not know. He tried to do a very large thing in the beginning, making friends with white men, and he was not allowed to go on with it. I thought that was dead inside of him and only now do I think that one day it may come alive again."

"I have thought of this too," Jeffords said soberly.

"My brother was Mangas Coloradas," she said. "There is no reason for me to love your kind. But wisdom does not need love. What my husband was trying to do before was right. With you he will try to do it again, maybe."

"It will take a very long time," he said quietly.

"It will take patience. But it has started — and you have done that."

"To try to change him is to try to change the shape of a steel blade," Jeffords said.

"It will not be a change," she said earnestly. "He was that way before. It will be only bringing him to himself again. Move slowly. Learn things. When the time comes, even if it is a long time from now, you may be able to do it."

"I hope so," Jeffords said.

"You came here for a purpose. He believes that all things are planned. One day you may be able to make him believe again that peace with the white people is planned. When he allows himself to believe that he will welcome it."

CHAPTER XVII

The Congress Hall was crowded. Jeffords and Silas St. John entered. Jeffords waved pleasantly to men he knew as he walked toward the bar. Some of the men returned the greeting. Others did not.

At the bar a man was about to lift a glass to his lips. His eyes fell on Jeffords. He set the glass down hard, untasted, and walked out of the saloon, his face dark and angry. Other men at the bar moved away a little so that Jeffords and his friend had a section of the bar to themselves.

Jeffords's eyes narrowed as he watched all this. He ordered whisky. The bartender pushed a bottle and two glasses toward him and then walked away. Jeffords filled the glasses. "What's going on here?" he asked St. John.

"Nothing."

"What's going on?" Jeffords asked again.

St. John fumbled unhappily with his glass. "You know how people are, Tom."

"How are they?"

"It's been too quiet here. They have nothing to do but talk among themselves."

"And what are they talking about?"

"The mail riders," St. John said.

Jeffords emptied his glass. "Let's have all of it."

"People are being killed right and left by Apaches."

"And the mail riders go through unharmed?"

"Some people don't like it, Tom."

Jeffords refilled his glass. "I was waiting for that to start."

"It will pass, Tom. It will pass."

"What else?"

"That's all. Just that."

Jeffords shook his head. "No, that isn't all. People wouldn't stop at that. There'd be a next step."

"That's all, Tom. Forget it."

Jeffords's face became hard and grim. "They wouldn't know why Cochise was keeping his word with me. They wouldn't believe an Indian could have that kind of honor. So they would figure that Cochise must be getting something out of it."

"Forget it, Tom," St. John said.

"Are they saying I've turned renegade?" Jeffords asked in a harsh voice.

St. John looked down at the bar. "Yes."

"And they must be saying that I'm selling Cochise

guns. That always goes with it. Are they saying that?"

"Some people are," St. John said.

A man burst into the saloon. His face was sweat-stained. He lurched stiffly to the bar. "Give me a drink, fast," he said in a parched voice.

"That's Ed Neely, from down Sonoita," St. John said. Jeffords drained his glass. "More trouble," he said.

Neely finished his drink. He turned his back to the bar and looked around the saloon. The talking stopped. Then Will Oury called out: "What's up, Ed?"

"Fort Buchanan," Neely said.

Oury walked up to the bar. "What about Fort Buchanan?" he asked. "They just finished rebuilding the place."

Neely nodded. "Cochise attacked it."

The news caused an uproar. Oury held up his hands for silence. "Buchanan? The troops just arrived there to garrison the place."

"Yes," Neely said. "Cochise was waiting, he was waiting all the time. He waited for the fort to be put up again and he waited for the soldiers to come and then he attacked it."

"What happened?" Oury said, looking at Jeffords.

"He drove out the soldiers. He burned the buildings again. He loaded up and he got away." Neely looked from face to face. "That man is a Napoleon, a Red Napoleon!"

Oury faced Jeffords. "You got anything to say about this?" he asked.

At that moment one of the mail clerks stuck his head into the saloon. "Captain Jeffords!" he called out.

Jeffords looked up. "Here I am."

"Mail rider just got in," the clerk said. He started to leave.

"Wait a minute," Oury shouted. The clerk stopped. "Did he have any trouble?"

The clerk grinned. "None at all."

As Jeffords walked out of the saloon, followed by St. John, he felt the eye of every man on him. He kept his hand close to his gun.

The mail riders continued to bear charmed lives. Their orders were to get the mail through and to keep out of trouble. It was as though they were invisible. Everywhere around them white men and Apaches fought, but they passed untouched. Jeffords became more and more a man apart. The pendulum had swung to the other extreme: from the hero who had gone alone to visit the dread Cochise, he had become the most friendless man in Tucson. Rumors that he was supplying Cochise with guns and liquor were repeated everywhere, but no one dared accuse Jeffords directly. His handiness with his gun was too well respected.

Jeffords exploded one day in his office: "I'm not making a cent out of this job! All over this country there is gold and silver — just waiting for a man to come along and dig it up. Why am I putting up with this nonsense!"

"You are getting the mail through," St. John said quietly.

Jeffords snorted. "So people can write letters telling how I sold out to the Indians?"

"It doesn't matter what they write," St. John said. "You

have been able to accomplish what no man in Arizona has been able to do. You have saved lives. You are keeping Tucson in touch with the rest of the country. Without you we would again become isolated." He looked earnestly at Jeffords. "You know, Tom, what people here say doesn't matter at all. You are performing a service for your country."

Jeffords nodded. "Yes," he said. "I know. I just have to let off steam now and then." Then he said: "You know, Silas, we're at war. We're at war with Cochise. A full-scale war. Staff officers planning campaigns, just the way they did in the Civil War! The biggest generals come out here and try to defeat this Indian! And they all fail. And they all go back to Washington, their tails between their legs." He bit off the end of a cigar. "Maybe a civilian can do what the army can't do," he said.

St. John was silent.

"It seems to have been written down for me," Jeffords said. "It seems that I was given one important thing to do in my life."

"To make peace with Cochise!"

Jeffords nodded. "I don't know how or when, but it's all I can think of. I know he wants it and I know it could be done. But it must be with honor on both sides. I believe Cochise would listen to my advice — but I would not ask him to come to one of these 'peace conferences' — the kind that end up with all the Indians dead."

St. John's eyes glowed. "If you could ever persuade Cochise to lay down his arms! What it would do for this country! If he stopped fighting the other Indians would stop too! They follow his lead in everything."

"It's a long road," Jeffords said.

"It may take years — but it would bring Arizona into its own! For farmers and ranchers and businessmen — people of peace. This started with the mails — but it would be bigger than the mails. It would be as big as the whole Territory."

Jeffords looked off into the distance. "Peace between the white man and the Indian. Living side by side — understanding each other. That's how this country started out a long time ago, Silas. A place where all kinds of people could live together, without fighting. They don't all have to believe in the same things. The only important thing is that they let other people believe what they please."

A week later a mail rider arrived in Tucson with an incredible story. He told it breathlessly to Jeffords and St. John. He had started out from Fort Bowie and a few miles after he left the fort he had come upon a fight between Indians and a wagon train.

"I know you gave out orders that we shouldn't get mixed up in fights like that, Captain Jeffords," the rider said. "But I just couldn't ride on without giving a hand to those white men. I tried to get to help them — but the Indians threw a rope around me and tied me to a tree.

"I figured it was curtains. I could imagine what was going to happen to me. I could feel the fire on my feet. The Indians left me there for about three hours. I watched while they killed every one of the travelers. They stripped the train of all its supplies and cut the horses and mules loose and set fire to the wagons. Then they came back to me and I began to say my prayers.

"Then a big, tall Indian — he looked like the boss — untied me. I never saw an Indian with a face like his. I felt his eyes were cutting holes into me. He put me back on my horse and then he slapped the horse and sent me on my way." He put the mailbag on a desk. "I got to get a drink, Cap!" he said in bewilderment. "Tied up after I started shooting at them and they let me go! I think maybe I even killed one of them — and they didn't do nothing to me."

He started for the door. St. John raised his hand to stop him. Jeffords shook his head. "Let him go."

"He'll make trouble," St. John said.

"We can't keep him locked up forever," Jeffords said. "He's going to talk sometime. Might as well get it over with."

Within fifteen minutes there were the sounds of voices outside the mail office. Jeffords lit a cigar, buckled on his gun and walked outside. Half a hundred men were collected, talking angrily. Jeffords said pleasantly: "Mail isn't ready yet. It will be in about an hour."

A man yelled: "How come the Indians didn't shoot your rider, Jeffords?"

"Yeah, what's going on between you and old Cochise?" another man demanded.

"What have you got against the rider?" Jeffords asked. "Would you rather have had him killed?" He stiffened as he saw Will Oury walking up. "Anything I can do for you, Oury?"

"People would like to know how come you and Cochise are such friends," Oury said quietly.

"Would they?"

"Nobody around here is fretting because your rider wasn't killed," Oury said. "Nobody wants the rider or any other white man killed. People only want a straight answer: What's between you and that red murderer?"

Oury stood indolently, his thumbs stuck into his belt. Jeffords felt his hand fall on his revolver. The talking got louder. A tall, red-faced youth, his mouth stained with tobacco juice, pushed his way forward. "We don't favor nobody who calls an Apache friend," the youth said.

Jeffords said: "My job is to see that the mail goes through. Nobody is getting hurt because of that. There were twenty-two riders killed when I first started. There hasn't been a man shot at since I had the talk with Cochise. That was all right with all of you. What's made you change your minds?"

The youth spat tobacco juice at Jeffords's feet. Jeffords pushed the cigar out of his mouth with his tongue. The youth glared up at him. "As Oury says, *Captain* Jeffords, we ain't complaining at all about your riders not getting shot. But there is something that stinks to high heaven about you making pals with an Apache. This town don't like renegades!"

Now the crowd moved back a little. Jeffords asked: "What did you say, mister?"

The young man opened his mouth to chew — and left it open. After several seconds his lips twitched.

"I asked you what you said," Jeffords repeated, his voice almost inaudible. His voice was so low that men in the back of the crowd could only see the movements of his lips.

The youth tried for a grin. "My tongue ran away," he said.

Jeffords sighed. His wrist suddenly felt cramped. He took his fingers away from his gun and flexed them. His forehead rippled with sweat.

Duffield shouldered his way through the crowd. "What in the name of jumping thunder is going on around here?" he bellowed. "I been hearing talk and I don't like it! It's been killing talk — and why Tom Jeffords ain't been doing some killing is more than I know. I been hearing crazy talk about him selling out to the Indians. That's a lie! I'm sick and tired about hearing it. As far as I can make out, Tom Jeffords don't need no help from me. He's the last man in town I'd want to have to draw against. But I'm saying this: from now on, talk against Tom Jeffords is talk against me. The next hombre who makes noises like an old woman will have to answer to Milt Duffield — as well as to him. Anybody who's got anything to say, say it right now!" He glared at the men. "All right," he said, "pull out of here! This is a United States government office — and there is work to be done!"

CHAPTER XVIII

The raid into Mexico was a success and the Indians took
many sheep and they returned to the Stronghold in good
spirits. They talked about the welcome their wives would
give them when they brought in their big haul.

Of them all, only Cochise was not happy. He took no
part in the good-natured chaffing and joking. He rode with
his head sunk low and he thought of the face of a Mexican he had killed in hand-to-hand combat and he felt tired
and his head was filled with rocks — as though the ghost
of the slain man were there, jumping back and forth.

A rider came up with the news that a party of white men,
eleven men and two wagons, was camped in a valley to the
north. The Indians gathered around Cochise. "Do we attack them?" Nahilzay asked.

Cochise saw Tahzay look at him questioningly. Cochise said: "Mexicans are good. White-eyes are better. We will attack."

He divided his warriors, sending half of them on a detour with the booty from Mexico, arranging where to meet them the next day. As he gave the orders, Cochise found he could not look at the face of his son. Then Tahzay asked if he could take command of the group leaving with the booty. Cochise regarded him silently. Then he nodded. He watched Tahzay ride away. It was not cowardice he knew. In the attack on the Mexicans, no one had been braver than Tahzay. It was just that he no longer desired to fight Americans. It was since Jeffords . . . Cochise thought.

With Nahilzay at his side, Cochise led his warriors to where the Americans were encamped. In the darkness they could make out the travelers sitting around a fire.

The Indians waited quietly through the night and Cochise tasted in advance the pleasure of the kill. The ache in his head would go away when the killing started, he thought.

At dawn he led the attack. Three of the Americans were killed immediately. Five others soon were picked off. The remaining three were captured alive and were bound to the wheels of the wagons, head down.

Brush was piled under the heads. Cochise knelt and watched and waited. The Indians worked at the old game without instructions. Nahilzay brought a torch to one of the piles of brush and looked at Cochise for the signal to go ahead. Then Cochise remembered the face of his son. He said: "Stop!"

The other Indians were suddenly silent. Cochise stood up. "Unbind them." Nahilzay did not move. "Unbind them," Cochise repeated.

Nahilzay put down the torch. He looked silently at Cochise for several moments. Then he freed the white man nearest him. The other Indians cut the bonds of the other two men.

Cochise said to the Indians: "Take everything you can carry." His voice was flat and toneless. When his men had selected everything they desired, Cochise said in the same voice: "Mount your horses." Without another word to the stupefied Americans, he jumped on his own horse and rode away.

The people celebrated the success of the raid. Cochise lay in his wickiup and listened to the sounds of the people. He could not bring himself to join the festivities. He remained alone and did not stir and the day changed into night and into day again.

He sent Tahzay to order a sweat-bath. Then the door of the wickiup opened. Jeffords entered. Cochise sat up. His face was haggard. "When did you come?"

"Just now."

Cochise walked outside. In the daylight his face looked more tormented than ever. His lips were dry and his eyes were red-rimmed. "I have ordered a sweat-bath," he said. "Share it with me."

Inside the bath house, Cochise stretched out and relaxed. His lean, powerful frame rested heavily on a slab of rock.

There was a new wound on his chest, memento of the raid. Cochise touched it lightly. "It could have been an important one," he said. He looked at his body. "The scars are old friends. Each one is a message." He touched the new one again. "Just a little closer and this might have been the final one. It could have started the long journey — and by now I would know the answers." He drew the steamy air into his lungs. "A man thinks too much about death. I believe death is not important. We die each day and when death comes at last it is always too late."

The sweat-bath boss threw some fresh water on the hot stones. They hissed. Steam filled the bath house and Jeffords could no longer see Cochise.

"An old woman once said that I would not live to be old and that I would not die in battle," Cochise said. His voice, through the steam, seemed to come from a long distance. "I have long waited for the bullet that would make her liar."

They lay in the steam-place for more than an hour and then they left, dripping with sweat, and walked to the stream and plunged into it. The water was like liquid ice. From behind a tree Nahilzay watched them, his eyes dark with hatred.

When Jeffords opened his eyes in the wickiup that night he had the feeling that he had been awake for some time. He was tense and he knew that his instincts were warning him that he was in danger. Then he heard the sound, the faintest of footfalls, and as he understood it, without conscious thought, moving automatically, he shifted slightly on the pallet, edging himself over to one side. And then there was a darkness, darker than the night, and he smelled something stale and there was a soft thud. He saw something gleaming and he stretched out and grabbed the wrist and forced back the knife.

He felt the wrist twist in his grasp, and he pushed himself upward and tried to get his attacker down. They rolled back and forth and Jeffords clung to the wrist. Then the man brought up his knee and smashed it into Jeffords's belly and Jeffords felt sick.

Jeffords groped with his left hand until he found the man's throat and he began to squeeze. The man twisted and tried to pull away. Jeffords's fingers closed on the throat like steel bars and then Jeffords heaved again and he was on top of the man and he had the man's arms stretched out on the ground and Jeffords raised his fist and brought it down like a hammer on the face that was turned up below him. He heard the bones break in the nose and the man made his first sound, a sharp, exhaling sound, and then he did not move any more.

Jeffords stood up warily. He lit his torch. Nahilzay was unconscious. His nose was bleeding. He was breathing noisily, little flecks of blood coming from his mouth. He held a long knife in his right hand. On the pallet where Jeffords had been sleeping there was a long slash.

There was another sound. Jeffords whirled. Cochise entered the wickiup, a shotgun in his hand. His eyes took in the scene instantly. He picked up a gourd of water and threw it on Nahilzay. Nahilzay stirred and opened his eyes.

He jumped to his feet. His mouth set into a tight line and he held himself proudly. His eyes asked for no mercy.

Cochise looked at Nahilzay with sorrow. He moved his head — and Nahilzay walked out of the wickiup. Cochise turned to follow him. Jeffords said: "No."

Cochise turned sharply. "This is not your affair."

"What are you going to do?"

"This does not concern you now."

"No one fights in my behalf," Jeffords said.

"Keep your silence," Cochise said sternly. "Do not interfere."

Jeffords understood the torment that was going on in Cochise's mind to make him speak in that manner. He put his hand on Cochise's shoulder. "This *is* my affair," he said. "Nahilzay tried to kill me — not you. Whatever the vengeance is, it is my vengeance."

"This is not vengeance," Cochise said. "This is punishment for a violation of my order."

"He attacked *me,*" Jeffords insisted.

"If it happened somewhere else it would be between you. Now the only important thing is that he tried to injure someone to whom I had given safety among my people. He must die — for making me into liar."

Through this talking Nahilzay stood outside the open door of the wickiup. He folded his hands across his chest. His face was without interest.

"I am no child to hide behind you, Cochise!" Jeffords said.

"In this place it is I who gives the orders." Cochise

turned to Nahilzay and now it was as though Jeffords were no longer there. "There has been none like you in battle," Cochise said to his war lieutenant. "Your life and mine were mixed often. Now it is ended." Then, as though commenting on some minor thing, Cochise said: "You should not have betrayed me."

He walked out of the dwelling, past Nahilzay. Nahilzay walked silently behind him. Jeffords rushed out.

Dawn was bringing its clear light. There was a chill in the air and a silence. Cochise walked across a clearing toward the place where the men shot arrows in the contests. At last Cochise stopped and faced Nahilzay. He said: "You are going to die. But why did you attack this man who has become my friend?"

"Since he has come to you he has blinded you," Nahilzay said. "He is turning you away from the ways of your race. He would make a 'tame' Apache of you. I do not fear to die. I regret only that my knife did not find its way to his heart first."

Now Jeffords strode up to Cochise. "Listen to me," he said, and now it was his voice that was stern. "It is my honor that is involved in this too. I am neither woman nor child who needs protection. This must be settled between Nahilzay and me!"

Cochise pondered and then he said: "Among us there are laws. This man has violated the greatest law — my word."

"No matter how you explain it, this is my business and I will settle it in my own way. This man has challenged me.

I accept the challenge. You have no right to order it otherwise."

Cochise looked first at Jeffords and then at Nahilzay. "How would you duel? He is less than you are with a gun. You are far less than he with the bow and arrow."

"He tried to kill me with a knife," Jeffords said. "A knife is good enough."

Cochise looked at the two men, closer to him than any other than his own sons. At last he said: "I have no right to deny you, Tagliato. But I say this: Nahilzay, you are no longer as a son to me. You may fight — but if you are victor, you will be banished from your people." Cochise looked at Jeffords. "You say that your honor is involved. That is enough, if you say it."

By now other Indians had wandered up and word passed quickly and soon almost the entire band had collected in the brightening morning. Cochise sent Tahzay to his wickiup and the youth returned with two knives with blades more than eight inches long.

Cochise examined the knives and then threw them point down into the earth. Teese handed Cochise his lance. Cochise drew a large circle on the ground, some fifteen feet in diameter. The knives were in the center.

Nahilzay stepped into the circle, his heels on the line Cochise had drawn. Jeffords removed his shirt and took a place on the line at the opposite side of the circle. Cochise held his lance extended, his face bitter, and then he lowered the lance and stepped back.

Nahilzay and Jeffords studied each other carefully. They

moved from side to side, to get the feel of the earth. Nahil-zay was the slenderer of the two but his chest was the deep barrel chest of an Apache warrior. His arms were long and sinewy. He moved as lightly as a cat.

Jeffords was less graceful. His motions were slower, more deliberate.

Suddenly, Nahilzay darted forward and picked up one of the knives. As he moved away his left foot flicked out and he tried to kick the other knife away. But as he had moved, so Jeffords had moved. The heel kicked into empty space and the other knife was secure in Jeffords's hand.

Then the two men moved back to the rim of the circle. Without any crouch to give him spring, Nahilzay leaped toward Jeffords, a lightning-swift leap that seemed to gather its momentum from nowhere. The knife twinkled in the morning light and Jeffords twisted only in time and saw the blade slide past him, missing him by inches. He whirled and with his left hand tried to strike Nahilzay down and with his right hand tried to get the knife into Nahilzay's body. Nahilzay twisted as he fell and darted under Jeffords's arm and in a moment was again at the far side of the circle.

The Indians murmured in their excitement.

Again Nahilzay leaped and in midair he seemed to change direction. He charged below Jeffords's waist, and he came in almost in a dive, his knife arm coiled. Jeffords struck out with his left hand and he struck Nahilzay on the neck, as a man kills a rabbit, and then he kicked out suddenly and kicked the knife from Nahilzay's hand. Nahilzay reached for it. Jeffords stepped on it.

Nahilzay straightened up and folded his arms. He looked at Jeffords contemptuously.

There was a long sigh from the Indians. By Indian law it now was Jeffords's right to attack the unarmed Nahilzay. Jeffords kicked the knife toward Nahilzay. The Indian bent down and picked it up and in the same move again leaped at Jeffords.

This time Jeffords was waiting for him. He held himself until just the last moment and then he shifted slightly and as Nahilzay passed he shot out his left arm and wrapped it around the Indian's waist, pinning Nahilzay's arms against his sides. He twisted the Indian around until Nahilzay was almost facing him and he lifted his right arm and brought it down hard and he felt the blade enter Nahilzay's back and he pushed down until the hilt stopped the blade from going deeper.

For a moment Nahilzay gave no sign of any kind. Holding him, Jeffords could feel the powerful resistance in his torso, still feel the attempt to pull the right arm from under his grip. The Indian's eyes were bright and glittering and then Nahilzay seemed to sag and his eyes clouded and a film covered them and his body became loose. Jeffords released him and the Indian fell down softly on the earth.

There was a long exhalation from the Indians, as though the sound came from a single mouth. Cochise walked into the circle and knelt before Nahilzay. He stood up. "The man is dead," he said. "The duel was fair. It is over and finished. None of this will remain in the heart of any man."

He pulled the knife from Nahilzay's back and picked up the knife that had fallen from Nahilzay's hand. He gave the knives to Tahzay. "Destroy these, my son," he said.

Nothing more was said of the fight or of the killing of Nahilzay. It was as though Nahilzay had never lived. His name was not spoken by Cochise. The other Indians acted toward Jeffords as they had before.

The night before he was to start back for Tucson, Jeffords sat before the fire with Cochise. The Apache pointed to the fire. "Tagliato," he said, "what do you see there?"

"A fire."

"Only a fire?"

Jeffords looked curiously at Cochise. The Indian was staring into the blaze with a strange expression on his face. "What do you see in the flames, Cochise?" Jeffords asked.

"A face," Cochise said.

"You have bad memories," Jeffords said.

"A memory." There was sudden uncanny fear in Cochise's eyes. "Tagliato, do you believe in ghosts?"

"A bad memory can become like a ghost," Jeffords said.

"I have a ghost. It lives with me." Cochise's hands twisted together. "It is the ghost of a Mexican I killed on this last raid. The face is there now, in the fire."

Something stirred in Jeffords's mind. Now, he thought, now it may be the time to say something.

"I saw him in a dream one night," Cochise said. "The door to my wickiup opened and he came in. I wanted to get up and fight him but I could not. I could just say: 'Ah, ah, ah.' I said: 'What do you want? Go away.' He stayed a long time and then I woke and I was wet with sweat."

"Can Nochalo not help you?"

"He made many ceremonies," Cochise said. "He has knowledge of ghost sickness. But he cannot help me. Sometimes it is in my head. It rocks there as though my head were filled with stones."

This may be the time to begin, Jeffords thought. "This is not just one man, maybe," he said.

"I see only one face."

"You think it is his face alone. His face is made of many faces. The face is the sum of all the things you would like to forget."

"There is nothing to forget," Cochise said harshly. "I have done only what I have had to do."

Jeffords reached out and put his arm on his friend's hand. "It is your whole time of hatred that is haunting you, Cochise," he said quietly.

"The path was made for me. I followed it." Cochise's face turned stony.

"You do not truly believe that," Jeffords said softly. "It was not so before. And you were happier then. There is a long line of dead faces."

"I did not start this war!"

"That is true. It was caused by a fool. But you know that it is a bad war. There will always be more white enemies. No matter how many of them you kill there will always be more. There are more white men than all the Apaches.

You can kill them every day and every night but in the end there will be more of them."

Cochise looked at him curiously. "Tagliato, you speak of your own people as 'them.' "

"I think with you, Cochise."

"I am not defeated!" Cochise said with sudden pride.

Jeffords nodded slowly. "You are a greater warrior than any one of them. But in the end they will defeat you. You have said this yourself. And now, while you are victorious in battle, you are becoming defeated inside yourself. I speak to you as a brother, Cochise."

The Indian was silent. He stared into the fire. Jeffords leaned closer to him. Jeffords said: "You are losing your war. You have less warriors now than you had six moons ago. Each harvest the ranks of the Chiricahua men becomes thinner. And you yourself are filled with the ghost sickness so that you see the face of a slain man in the fire."

Cochise was silent for a long while. Then he asked: "What else can be done? What else is offered to us? Are we offered a peace with justice? Are there honest men to treat with?" He shook his head. "No, Tagliato, there is nothing but treachery." He turned his head so that his burning eyes were on Jeffords. "What does the white man say we can have? A reservation? What is a reservation? A large jail where the Indians starve and go cold. The Navajos made a peace with the white men in New Mexico and the white men betrayed them and put them in the Canyon de Chelly and half of the Navajos perished. Look around everywhere, Tagliato. Show me one reservation where the Indians are treated justly, where they can live in the dignity that is befitting to men."

"The fault lies not with the reservations, maybe, but with the men who administer them," Jeffords said slowly.

"Do you think that can be it?" Cochise asked. "There might be hope if it were that."

"The way things are, each agent is supreme boss," Jeffords said. "A reservation is just as good — or just as bad — as the agent who runs it. If you had a good agent — you could have a good reservation."

"Maybe." Cochise was not convinced. "But why must there be a reservation?"

"Until there is peace between the Indian and the white man it is necessary to keep them separated. One bad white man or one bad Indian could undo all the work good Indians and good white men have done."

Cochise looked at him mockingly. "Then why not put the white men on reservations? This is our country."

Jeffords was silent. Cochise smiled painfully. He said: "No, Tagliato, I have my own burden to carry. I would rather see all my people dead than deliver them to the white soldiers. You are a true brother. I will listen to you as I listen to myself. But there is no answer to our problem. We will not conquer. But we will die like men."

He faced the fire again. Jeffords watched the reflection of the flames on the lined, tired face. Cochise said: "I will not die of hunger because the white man will not give me food. The Chiricahuas are not beggars. We need no one to give us food and clothing and shelter — as charity. We will take

[202]

what we need to live and if we get killed — well, a man can do worse than die in battle. At least I will not die of a bullet in my back while I sleep. Mangas Coloradas lived to be an old man — and died that way. It would have been better for him to have died fighting, a gun in his hand, a bullet in his chest." He shook his head heavily. "A bullet hurts more when it enters from the back."

The men sat quietly and the night wind rose and the fire crackled.

Cochise seemed to go into a revery. "It would be a good thing if all men spoke with a straight tongue, Tagliato," he said. "Why do men not speak without lying?"

"I do not know, Cochise."

"A man should never lie."

"No, he should not. But a great many do."

"That is true," Cochise said. "But they need not do it. If a man asks you or me a question we do not want to answer we simply say: 'I do not want to talk about that.' But many men lie."

CHAPTER XIX

During the months that followed, Jeffords divided his time between Tucson and any place where Cochise established a rancheria.

Gradually he came to be regarded in Tucson as a man of mystery. Many stories were told about him. It was said by some that he was seen with Cochise on raids. Men believed that he supplied the Apaches with guns, although everyone knew that it was impossible to get anything as bulky as a shipment of guns into Tucson without everybody's knowing about it.

He kept his mail office running smoothly and efficiently

and Cochise kept his pledge to the letter: mail riders never were attacked. The people of Tucson accepted the situation for what it was. It was not a time or a place where men asked questions of other men, and Tom Jeffords was known to be a dangerous man on the draw.

In his thinking, Jeffords came almost to be more Indian than white man. He understood the problems of the Apaches more plainly than he did his own. As time went on he grew even closer to Cochise. He developed a vast respect for the deep, complicated mind of the Apache chief. He found that when Cochise was not under the spell of one of his frequent moods of depression, he could lift his mind to great heights. He found Cochise witty, kind, a man of compassion and understanding. When he could, Jeffords spoke to Cochise about peace. Cochise listened. It was all Jeffords could ask for, to begin with — that Cochise should listen to him.

In time, Jeffords hoped, Cochise might do more than listen.

Late one afternoon, after they closed the mail office for the day, Jeffords and St. John walked to the Congress Hall. The streets of the Old Pueblo were crowded. Soldiers ogled Mexican girls. Men slept in the plaza.

The saloon was crowded, as usual. An epidemic of malaria had been sweeping through Tucson and men thought whisky was the best medicine for the disease. Jeffords walked to the bar, looking neither to the right nor the left. He knew that many eyes were on him and that men were whispering.

He stood at the bar, drinking quietly with St. John. A man staggered in. At first Jeffords thought he was drunk. Then he saw that he was not drunk at all.

The man was followed by other men. All were cursing. The first man reached the bar and asked for a drink. One of the men who had followed him in said loudly: "Tell what happened, Deke."

Deke finished another drink before he spoke. He was a rancher from Sonoita. He had been working his field. The Indians came. As he spoke he stared out into space as though he were seeing it all over again. The Indians killed his wife and his children and set fire to his house. The first thing he had known about it was when he had seen the smoke from the house. By the time he got there the Indians were gone. He got on his horse and went after them. He didn't care about staying alive — but he wanted to take some of the red devils with him. He never caught up with them.

He spoke as though his mouth were a hollow cave. "What do I do now?" he asked of no one in particular.

A heavy-set man with a two-day stubble of beard on his face banged the bar with his fist. He was Les Hawkins, a rancher near Pantano, whose place had been raided by Apaches two weeks before. He pushed people aside until he reached Jeffords. He pointed angrily at Jeffords, and shouted: "Why don't you ask him?"

Deke, in a daze, sidled up to Jeffords. "What do I do now, mister?" he asked. "Can you tell me?"

"He can tell you," Hawkins said. "He knows all about Indians."

The other men, sensing a gun fight, began to move back. Jeffords looked steadily at Hawkins. He spoke to Deke but he never stopped looking at Les Hawkins. "The Indians who raided your place ought to be put to death," Jeffords said.

Hawkins roared. "Listen to him! Go ahead, Deke, ask him whether *he* would help catch them and string them up."

"The Indians ought to be killed," Jeffords repeated evenly. "Then some of the white men who made them the way they are ought to be killed too. Then maybe we could start all over again."

"What white men made them what way?" Hawkins shouted. "What the devil are you trying to say, Jeffords?"

"I think you've been drinking too much," Jeffords said.

"That's my business. I drink like a white man."

Jeffords cocked his head.

"I do everything like a white man," Hawkins said.

"You might quit talking," Jeffords said.

Hawkins's hand went to his gun. Jeffords moved faster. Jeffords fired. Hawkins spun around, a bullet in his right arm. Jeffords looked at the other men in the bar. "This thing isn't Deke," he said bitterly. "Those Indians ought to be strung up — same as anybody who kills without cause.

But has anybody here tried to figure out why Indians started killing Americans in the first place?"

He strode out of the room. He went to the place he lived and packed his few belongings. St. John came in. "What are you doing, Tom?" he asked.

"I'm moving out." Jeffords's face was crossed with pain. "I don't belong here," he said. "I don't know where I belong. I don't belong to my own people."

"Where are you going?"

"I don't know." He threw the pack over his shoulders. "I've been cooped up in one place too long. I almost killed a man tonight. It will get worse. The more Cochise keeps his word with me the more it's going to make people mad. If I stay here there will be killings." He looked at St. John, his eyes dark with bitterness. "I got to find out where I belong and who I belong to, Silas. My own people think I'm a renegade and I can't live like an Indian." He held out his hand. "Take care of things," he said.

Tom Jeffords drifted over to New Mexico and moved aimlessly from place to place for many months. He shaved off his beard. He tried to hide from himself. He did not know what to believe. Who was right? he asked himself. And no matter who it was who was right, how was it going to end?

In the early spring of 1870 he was sitting in a saloon in Mesilla in New Mexico Territory. An army captain walked up to him. "Mind if I join you in a drink, Captain Jeffords?" the captain asked.

"Sit down."

"My name is Farnsworth." He was a tall, gray-eyed man.

"You seem to know my name."

"I inquired about you."

"Why?"

"I need a scout, Captain Jeffords."

CHAPTER XX

The wanderings of Jeffords had been watched over by
Cochise, whose men were everywhere. The Apache leader
received regular reports about the man he loved as a
brother. When he heard that Jeffords had cut off his beard,
he smiled sadly at Tahzay, saying: "He tries to change his
face."

"He who saw him says that it makes him into a different
man," Tahzay said.

"It is not that easy," Cochise said. "His people turned
against him and that is the worst thing that can happen to

a man. Now he tries to find another body to live in, but it is not that easy. The beard will not be there, but the man is the same."

One day Tahzay came to his father in great excitement. "Nantan Jeffords has joined the soldiers of an American officer named Farnsworth!" he said. "He is serving him as scout against the Indians in New Mexico!"

To Tahzay's astonishment, Cochise nodded in satisfaction. "The news is good, my son," he said.

"Good news? That Nantan Jeffords leads soldiers against Indians?"

"It is the beginning of his getting well. He is finding himself again."

Tahzay was utterly bewildered. "But he is your enemy!"

"He and I cannot be enemies," Cochise said. "He is only returning to life."

"What if he leads troops here?"

"We will fight them," Cochise said.

"You and Nantan Jeffords shooting at each other?"

Cochise nodded, his eyes alight with understanding. "Why not, my son?" he asked. "It would not matter. The important thing is that he no longer runs away. That is the bad thing. It is worse than getting killed."

"Why does he join with white men who called him renegade?" Tahzay asked, still unable to understand.

"You must try to see it," Cochise said. "They are his people. A man has to live with his people. You must understand these things. Once you will sit in my place and your understanding must go beyond you — it must enter into all things. Try to look past what a man does, to see the reason for his doing it. If the man is a friend, then the reason is more important than the action."

Jeffords rode into the Stronghold. When Cochise greeted him they stood silently and looked at each other. It was almost a year since they had seen each other.

Cochise studied the clean-shaven face. He thought the lack of beard made Jeffords look younger. Then he looked at his eyes. The pain that was there filled him with sadness.

"How are you, Cochise?" Jeffords asked.

"Nothing has changed, Tagliato."

Jeffords shook his head. "Much has changed. I have come here to tell you I have agreed to serve as a military scout for soldiers in New Mexico."

"Because a man must take sides in a war," Cochise said.

"I will be many miles from here. There is little chance that we would meet — in battle," Jeffords said. The words came out hard. "But there is that chance. I may become a danger to you." He raised his head and looked at Cochise. "I am your prisoner, Cochise."

"It is a long time since you spoke my language," Cochise said mildly. "It is difficult for me to understand you."

Jeffords chuckled softly. "You understand me. You understand everything."

"We talked of this before, a long time ago," Cochise said. "We knew it might be this way one day."

"And now it is that day."

[212]

"Tell me, are we still the same, you and I, one to the other?" Cochise asked.

"Yes, Cochise."

"Then we fight each other!" Cochise's eyes suddenly were shining. "All right, we fight each other — but as brothers. I have told you your bullet would not hurt as much as another's."

Jeffords waited until he could speak. "Things should have been different. What we could have done together!"

"No one does anything," Cochise said. "We think we do things. But we do not. We sit and watch things get done. Sometimes we even think we can change things — but we can not. Everything has been decided. All we do is sit and watch it happen."

"Do you believe that truly, Cochise?"

"There is a path for everyone. Maybe we can move a little from side to side, but it is always within the path. I saw the path of my people a long time ago. It is a path leading to the edge of a cliff. We all walk the same path and soon we will have to go over the cliff. Some soon — some later. It does not matter."

"That is how fighting is," Jeffords said. "Men moving like sheep against each other. The reasons are forgotten but the fighting still goes on."

"Men will fight," Cochise said very simply. "Men will always fight. If there were no white men we would fight other Indians — or Mexicans. If there were no Indians your soldiers would find someone else to fight. Everything that lives, fights. From the smallest to the largest. That is

[213]

how it is intended. Each thing lives on that which is weaker. By destroying other living things he makes his own place in the forest safer."

"The forest is big enough for everyone, maybe," Jeffords said.

"Each always wants the place where the other is standing."

"And the end?"

Cochise gestured widely with his hands. "The weak always lose. For a long time we were the strong. Now we are the weak. We will die. Slowly — on reservations — or swiftly — in battle. But we will die. Then it will be your turn." He embraced his friend. "It was good that you came here. We still speak to each other with a straight tongue. Listen to me. I knew of your decision to become an army scout before you came here. We still stand higher to each other than our peoples stand to each other."

"That is true, Cochise."

"And now we will become brothers."

"We are brothers, Cochise."

"We will become blood brothers. We will mix our blood."

Jeffords eyes widened. "Now? When I leave you to become your enemy?"

"Now, Tagliato — when you are as close to me as my own sons."

Jeffords breathed out hard. "You are a great man, Cochise. You are a very great man."

"It is our brotherhood," Cochise said.

In the night, Nochalo prepared the ceremony.

Cochise and Jeffords knelt, facing each other, and chosen warriors sat in a small circle around them. Nochalo stepped inside the circle and set down two goblets covered with markings. There was no sound. For this ceremony there were no singers or musicians.

Nochalo said: "What a man is is in his blood." He lighted a small fire and held the tip of the knife in the flames. He said: "The quality of the man — the things of his body — the things of his head — the things of his heart and his soul — all are in the blood."

He took the right wrists of each man. He said: "In each drop of blood there is all of the man. There is everything he thinks and everything he feels. A man is made of his blood, which he got from his father, which his father got from his father — which each man gives to his son, and which his son gives to his son."

He released his grip on the wrists and took the heated blade from the fire. He waved the knife to all the directions and then he plunged it into the earth. He said: "The blood is in the man. And the earth is his mother."

He took the knife from the earth and he cut open the flesh on Cochise's right arm eight inches above the wrist and he held the arm over one of the goblets and allowed the blood to fall into it. Then he took Jeffords's right arm and opened the flesh eight inches above his wrist and held the arm over the other goblet and let the blood fall into it.

Now Nochalo held the two arms together so the cuts

covered each other and the blood mixed. He held them together for a long while. He closed his eyes and prayed. Then he released the arms and he said: "Drink."

Cochise and Jeffords each picked up the cup which had the blood of the other and drank.

As Jeffords prepared to return to Mesilla the next day he said to Cochise: "When I come back alone I come as friend. If I come with others — I am an enemy."

"We no longer are friends, Sheekasay," Cochise said, calling Jeffords by the Apache word for "brother" for the first time. "We now are blood brothers."

CHAPTER XXI

Captain Farnsworth dismissed his troops on the parade ground at garrison headquarters in Tulerosa in the western part of the New Mexico Territory. He leaned wearily on his saddle horn and then he said to Tom Jeffords: "Well, another scouting party and the same bad luck." He sighed. "Looks like the Apaches outsmarted us again."

"We have exactly the wrong number of troops here," Jeffords said. "We have too few to do a real job and too many to have them sit around doing nothing."

Farnsworth dismounted. "Let's go get a drink, Tom. I think I swallowed a peck of dust, at least, this trip."

Jeffords climbed down slowly. "Maybe you ought to get yourself another scout, Captain. I don't seem to be doing you much good."

Farnsworth looked at him quickly. "We're doing better

[217]

than any other company in the Territory, Tom," he said earnestly. "Nobody could do what you have done. It's not your fault that the Apaches seem to be directed by a military genius." He paused and said reflectively, "You know, Tom, in his way this Cochise really is a kind of Red Napoleon. He seems to know what we are going to do all the time. Everything works for him."

"He once told me he has little birds who tell him things," Jeffords said.

"And now he has 'little birds' telling things to the Mimbres Apaches too," Farnsworth said. He regarded Jeffords keenly. "You have a great deal of respect for Cochise, haven't you, Tom?"

"A great deal, Captain, a very great deal."

Farnsworth nodded. "I know what you mean. I'm beginning to have some of it myself."

The men entered the club. They stood at the bar and washed the dust of the road from their throats. A few moments later a man rose from a group of officers seated around a table and approached them. Jeffords looked at him curiously. He was a tall, white-bearded man in the uniform of a general. His right arm was missing, and the right sleeve of his uniform was neatly pinned up.

The general walked up to Jeffords. "My name is General Howard. Is this Mr. Jeffords?"

"That is my name," Jeffords said.

"Can you take me to the camp of the Indian, Cochise?" General Howard asked quietly.

Jeffords's blue eyes became very clear. "General Howard.

I remember hearing about a General Oliver Otis Howard — a great hero in the Civil War," he said.

"I fought in the Civil War, Mr. Jeffords."

"General Howard — the Christian General, he was called."

Howard smiled. "I have heard that name applied to me."

"Who sent you here, sir?" Jeffords asked.

"The President of the United States," Howard said.

"Everybody is responsible to the President," Jeffords said.

"I am responsible to President Grant directly, Mr. Jeffords. I have come here as a personal representative of General Grant to treat with Cochise."

Jeffords gripped the bar hard. "And what powers do you have, sir?"

"I have full powers, Mr. Jeffords. And I have been told that you are the one man in the Southwest who can take me to see Cochise."

A strange look appeared on Jeffords's face. "Will you go there with me without soldiers, General?"

"Yes, Mr. Jeffords, if that is necessary."

Captain Farnsworth protested instantly. "That would be most dangerous, sir. You must take a military escort with you."

Jeffords and Howard continued to measure each other. Then Jeffords said quietly: "If you go with soldiers you will need an army, General, and that will only mean a continuation of the war." He could not hide the sudden eagerness in his eyes. "If you go with me it may be that I can help you make a peace with him."

Howard nodded. "I will go alone with you, as you suggest, sir," he said. He raised his hand as Farnsworth and other officers again began to protest. "Furthermore, Mr. Jeffords, you will be in complete command." He bowed slightly. "I am under your orders, sir."

"Yes," Jeffords said, almost to himself, remembering his old dream — a peace, and a peace with honor, for his country and for Cochise. "Yes," he repeated.

"Would you be good enough to accompany me to my quarters, Mr. Jeffords, so that we may make our plans?" the general asked.

When they entered the general's tent, Howard excused himself. He picked up a small, worn Bible. He read silently from it for a few minutes. Jeffords found himself deeply impressed. He removed his hat and watched the movement of Howard's lips.

Howard put the Bible down. "What do you suggest, Mr. Jeffords?"

"There is an Indian named Chee," Jeffords said. "He is the son of Mangas Coloradas. I will try to find him. He is supposed to be not far from here. There is another young warrior named Ponce. I will ask them both to help us."

"I will do whatever you suggest," Howard said.

On the twentieth day of September, 1872, General Howard, Tom Jeffords, Captain J. A. Sladen, Howard's aide-de-camp, and a couple of packers left Tulerosa. That night Jeffords left the group at the camp they had made and he disappeared. He returned the next day with the son of Mangas Coloradas.

Jeffords watched keenly as Howard greeted Chee. The general shook hands gravely with the Indian warrior. Chee searched the face of Howard and then he turned his eyes to Jeffords and Jeffords could see in them the light of approval.

The next day, while crossing one of the tributaries of the Rio Grande, Jeffords picked up a fresh track of horses. "A rider has come to the brow of that hill," he said to Howard. "He saw us and turned back. We'll follow."

They rode until they came to a steep descent leading to a gorge. At the base of the gorge flowed the Rio Conchinillo Negro. On the bank of the river was a small Indian camp.

"There is Ponce," Jeffords said. He spurred his horse and rode rapidly to his old friend. Ponce embraced him and after the two men spoke, Jeffords returned to General Howard. "He says he will come with us — but he wants to know who will take care of his little band," Jeffords said. He winked at Howard. "And he says that his horse is not good enough to keep up with ours."

"We can satisfy him," Howard said.

The band was brought to a nearby hamlet and Howard ordered that the Indians be given a thirty-day ration of food. He then gave Ponce his own spare horse.

The next morning Ponce appeared, ready to accompany them. He was on foot.

"Where is the horse I gave you?" Howard asked.

"I had to give him to my wife," Ponce said innocently.

Since Howard had no other spare horse, he told Ponce they would share the same animal. From then on Ponce either rode behind the general — or else Howard or Ponce walked. Jeffords missed none of this. The more he saw of Howard the more he felt that perhaps the right man had come at last to make a peace with Cochise.

The twenty-third of September was spent at Fort Bayard and supplies were replenished. Then the group left for the next stop, Silver City. Their arrival had a frightening effect on the residents of that community. Upon seeing the two Apaches, miners barred their doors and took down their rifles. Angry men accosted the group and demanded that the Indians be turned over to them for hanging. Howard ordered the miners to disperse. Then he bade Chee and Ponce to stay close to him.

Ten miles from town, the next morning, a party of prospectors rode up to them. One of the miners, a man whose brother had recently been slain by Apaches, lifted his rifle immediately and aimed it at Chee. Howard rode between them. "You will have to kill me first," he said.

The prospector lowered his rifle. Cursing, he rode away. Chee put his arm on Howard's shoulder and held it there for a moment.

"You have a friend who will never forget you," Jeffords said to the general.

In the camp that night Howard finished his daily reading

of the Bible and then he asked Jeffords: "If Cochise agrees to make peace, will he live up to his word?"

"If he gives his word he will keep it."

"Is there anything I should know before I talk to him, Mr. Jeffords?" Howard asked.

Jeffords thought for a little while. "Don't make any promises you can't keep, General. If you promise him ten things and give him only nine he will remember you as the man who failed to give him the tenth thing. It would be better to promise less — and give more. I don't know how well you know Apaches, General, but they keep their word, to the letter. As far as I know, Cochise has never violated his word. If you do as well— there may be a peace."

Howard held his hand before the fire. The light flickered on his long white beard. He looked, Jeffords thought, like one of the patriarchs out of the Bible he read so frequently and so devoutly.

"You have known Cochise for a long time, have you not, Mr. Jeffords?" Howard asked.

"A long time, General."

"And you have great respect for him."

"Yes."

"Mistakes have been made, Mr. Jeffords. I would like to have some of your ideas about what can be done to make right old wrongs." When Jeffords did not reply, Howard said earnestly: "Treatment of the Indians cannot be improved without the co-operation and good will of those white men who know Indians best. If there is anything you can tell me, Mr. Jeffords, it is your duty to your friend, Cochise, and to your government, to tell it to me."

Jeffords stared into the fire. Then he looked suddenly at Howard. The general's face was calm and serene and Jeffords saw wisdom and compassion in his eyes. "Before a man is sent out to take charge of Indians he ought to find out something about them," Jeffords said. "He ought to have to study the language — the religion and traditions. I know Cochise. He has more pride than a regiment of cavalrymen. He's honest and he has dignity and he is a king among his own people. We never tried to understand that. Most of the people out here look on him as a red savage — better off dead. Well, there have been millions of dollars lost and thousands of people killed and wounded because we didn't try to understand him. Now you have to come out here — a personal ambassador from the President of the United States, to straighten things out. A second lieutenant with horse sense could have done that twelve years ago. Just as a second lieutenant started it."

Howard's eyes were filled with understanding. "I think we do not disagree, Mr. Jeffords. My answer to what you say is this: in our haste to conquer this new country we have forgotten the teachings of the Saviour — and we have had to pay."

"The Apache Indians believe in God too," Jeffords said.

"Their beliefs are equally holy in the eyes of the Lord."

Jeffords stood up. "If you really believe that, General, maybe you are the man I have been waiting for all these years."

CHAPTER XXII

The men rode for days. Howard and Jeffords held long conversations and Jeffords spoke of many things that had been on his mind for a long time. Howard was a man who would listen.

The group wound around the sandhills and the waste places of southwestern New Mexico until they came in sight of the Peloncillo Mountains. There Chee rode ahead of the others and made small fires, in a circle.

Ponce said to Howard in explanation: "Peace, smoke of peace."

A little later Chee barked like a coyote. He was answered by a similar sound from the mountainside. He scurried up the slope and another Apache suddenly appeared, as though out of the earth. Ponce waved to the group to follow. They came to a spring. They found some Indians there.

"One of Cochise's small bands," Jeffords said.

"Is Chief Cochise nearby?" Howard asked.

"I don't think so. He has rancherias scattered everywhere," Jeffords said. He rode up to the Indians, who recognized him and greeted him with excitement. He saw Skinyea and hugged him warmly. After he spoke to Skinyea he returned to Howard. "Cochise is still a hundred miles away," he said. "Do you want to go on?"

"I have come to see him," Howard said quietly. "Of course we will continue on."

"I think you will have to get rid of the packers now," Jeffords said. "I told you we would have to travel alone."

"May Captain Sladen accompany me?"

"No one else," Jeffords said.

The next morning, Howard, Jeffords and Sladen started out again with Chee and Ponce. They entered the Chiricahua Mountains and went up a steep ascent on a trail so blind Howard and Sladen could make nothing of it. That day the men rode forty miles over the Chiricahuas.

The heat was intense. The rocks radiated heat like an open oven. Of them all, General Howard, the oldest, showed the discomfort the least. In his full uniform, he rode with martial pride, uncomplaining.

The next day was equally cloudless. The heat seemed to get worse. The men crossed the Sulphur Spring Valley. Jeffords pointed ahead. "Those are the Dragoons, General," he said. "In those mountains Cochise has his Strongholds."

In the late afternoon the men reached the old Butterfield station in the valley. They decided to rest there. A small guard of soldiers was stationed in the depot. The soldiers were flabbergasted to see a general arrive with so little ceremony.

The men shared their rations and Howard lay down for a nap. He noticed Chee edging away nervously from three dogs which were snarling at him. "Come and sleep with me, Chee," Howard said gently.

Chee ran over to him and lay down and Howard spread his army greatcoat over both of them and they slept. Jeffords gazed in wonder at the American general and the Apache Indian sleeping side by side.

Shortly after midnight, Jeffords woke Howard and they resumed their ride. They passed through the Middle March Pass in the Dragoons. They came to a cool, swiftly flowing mountain stream and Jeffords called a halt. The men and the animals rested through the day.

Soon after camp was made, Chee disappeared. Ponce made fires in a circle. While the men were eating supper, two Indians, no more than boys, came down from the hills.

"They are coming from the Stronghold," Jeffords said to Howard. "I think we will not have long to wait."

Without speaking, the boys seated themselves and helped themselves to food. When they had eaten their fill they pointed to a gap behind them and they said that Chee had sent them and that he wanted them to come up to one of the Apache rancherias.

The men started out again. It was the old familiar route to Jeffords. He rode in silence, recognizing every foot of the way, each rock, each tree, each turn in the trail. And then, before his eyes, appeared the wickiups of the Stronghold. And the Indians recognized him and they shouted his name.

Soon Chee appeared. He said that Cochise was in the other Stronghold. Jeffords led the men to the stream, and there, under a tree, they made camp.

Howard spread out his blanket. "Will I have time for a little rest, Mr. Jeffords?" he asked.

"Yes, General. I will call you."

"Thank you, Mr. Jeffords." Howard took out his Bible and read from it by the light of a small candle. Then he lay down on the blanket. "Will there be peace, Mr. Jeffords?"

"I do not know," Jeffords said.

As Howard made himself comfortable, several Indian children walked up to him and stared at him curiously. One lay down at Howard's feet. When Howard did not shoo the child off, others snuggled up against him. They lay there like contented puppies.

Howard smiled. "This does not mean war, Mr. Jeffords," he said. He slept.

In the morning the men ate breakfast and waited. Howard asked Jeffords: "Does Cochise know that we are here?"

Jeffords smiled. "He has known exactly where we have been for some time."

At that moment Ponce jumped to his feet. "Someone is coming!" he shouted.

A single horseman was riding slowly down a ravine. Jeffords said with some excitement: "It is Tahzay, son of Cochise!"

Tahzay rode up to Jeffords. He jumped from his horse. He put his arms around the tall white man. He spoke to Jeffords and then Jeffords said to Howard: "Cochise will be here in a few minutes."

Five minutes later Cochise came down the ravine. He entered the rancheria slowly. He climbed down from his horse. He turned his back on Howard and held Jeffords tightly in his arms. He said: "Sheekasay, it lightens my heart to see you again."

"My brother," Jeffords said.

Cochise turned with great dignity until he faced Howard. His features became hard and his lips compressed.

"This is Cochise," Jeffords said to the general.

Howard held out his hand. "Good day, señor," he said in Spanish.

Cochise accepted the hand. He did not reply.

Tahzay folded a blanket and his father sat down on it. Tahzay took his place at his side. Howard and Sladen and the other men arranged themselves in a small circle.

Cochise asked Jeffords: "Is this a good man?"

"I believe so," Jeffords said.

"How long have you known him?"

"Almost a moon."

"Can he be trusted?"

"I do not know, but I believe so."

"Will he do what he says he will?"

"I do not know," Jeffords said quietly. "I think he will. I cannot be sure, but I think he will."

"Enju," Cochise said. "It is enough that *you* brought him to me."

Then he spoke at great length to Chee and Ponce. They told him in detail of their own experience with Howard and of their impressions of him.

Cochise turned his head to Howard and spoke. Jeffords translated for him. "Cochise says will the general explain the object of his visit."

"The President of the United States sent me to make peace between Cochise and the white people," Howard replied.

When Jeffords translated this, Cochise replied: "Nobody wants peace more than I do."

General Howard said with emphasis: "Then, as I have full power, we can make peace."

Cochise's black eyes burned into the old soldier. Howard felt as though Cochise were seeing what was inside his head. Without removing his gaze, Cochise again began to speak. He spoke for more than an hour, pausing often so Jeffords could change the words into English. As always, when he turned his mind over the treacherous things done to his race, Cochise could not retain his calm. His voice rose and fell harshly and he gestured angrily.

"I know of these things," Howard said when Cochise was done. "There are two kinds of people in the United States. One is friendly to the Indians. The other is hostile to them. The friends of the Indians now are in power and General Grant is the leader of these good Americans."

"And later," Cochise replied quickly. "If the bad people come to power — what happens to us then?"

"If the Indians prove they are friends they will have nothing to fear," Howard said. As Cochise's lips curled slightly, Howard said: "Believe me, O Cochise, we are not a bad people. We have been stupid and thoughtless, perhaps, but we are not bad. You have seen the worst of us. When Americans do wrong things, when they break the laws of their country, they go to distant places — just as bad Indians do. You have seen many of these bad Americans. But that is not how our country was formed. In the beginning, many good Americans came to this country from places across a great ocean to escape from bad governments and bad rulers. These good Americans understand what it is to be persecuted for their religion and their political beliefs — for many things. These good Americans can learn to look upon the Indians as brothers and to live by their side in peace."

Nothing the general said, not a single inflection in his voice, escaped the ears of Cochise.

"I would like to persuade you to bring your people to

a fertile land on the Rio Grande," Howard continued. "I would like to bring all the Apaches there and give them as much land as they need to support themselves to live in peace with dignity."

Now Cochise shifted his attitude and settled down to bargain. "I have been there," he said without interest. "That move will break up my tribe because my people do not like it there. Why not give me Apache Pass? Give me that and I will protect all the roads. I will see that nobody's property is taken by the Indians."

"Perhaps we can do that," General Howard agreed.

Cochise asked suddenly: "How long will you stay here?"

"I came from Washington to see you and to make peace," Howard said. "I will stay until that is done."

Cochise pondered for a little while. Then he said to Jeffords: "I will see how much of a friend of the Indian he really is." He said to Howard: "My people are out making a living. I will send for them so that we may all talk. If they come across any whites there will be a fight and people will be killed on both sides. I want you to go to Fort Bowie tonight and tell the soldiers not to shoot my people as they come here."

"I will send Captain Sladen to Fort Bowie to notify the commander there," Howard said.

"The soldiers may not obey Captain Sladen," Cochise said. "They will obey you."

Howard rubbed his face wearily. He said to Jeffords: "I am very tired. I do not know how to get to Bowie from here."

"I think you ought to do as he says," Jeffords said. "He wants to know how much to trust you. The Indians will show you a new route to Bowie. You can make Sulphur Spring, about twelve miles from here, direct, sleep there, go to Bowie tomorrow and return in about three days."

"If you think it will help, Mr. Jeffords, I am ready to go," the general said.

Jeffords felt a sudden, strong sympathy for the tired old man. "I believe it will, General," he said.

"Then inform Cochise that I will do as he asks."

"I will call my people," Cochise said. "It will take about ten days to get them together." He stood up and walked away. Later he returned, followed by women bearing food and drink. He said to Howard: "We were once a large people, covering these mountains. One day my best friend, Mangas Coloradas, was seized by an officer of the white men and was killed by treachery."

"There are many white men who are bad," Howard replied. "There are differences between us — as there are among your people."

"The worst place of all is Apache Pass," Cochise said grimly. "There six Indians, one my brother, were murdered and their bodies were hung up. Now Americans and Mexicans kill an Apache on sight. I have struck back with all my might. My people have killed Americans and have taken their property. I have killed ten white men for every Indian who was slain — but I know that the whites are many and that the Indians are few."

His dark eyes became somber. "Why must the Indians

be shut up on reservations? We will make peace. We will keep it faithfully. But let us go around as free Americans."

When Howard replied his voice was heavy with sorrow. "Hear me out, O Cochise. This country is large. It does not belong entirely to the Indians, although the Indians were here first. All the children of God have an interest here. But until there is trust — complete trust — on both sides, there must be some control.

"To keep peace we must fix boundaries. A peace such as you propose would not last a week. Suppose that some rough prospectors should fire upon your people and kill some of them. Or suppose that some of your warriors would take the life of a white man. Then the peace would be hopelessly broken."

He shook his head slowly. "No, believe me, a reservation is not a prison. It is as much for the protection of the Indian as it is anything else. There you will be safe and secure and your families can grow and your young men will not be troubled and your children will not be endangered. I know how many bad Americans have mistreated Indians on other reservations, but I pledge you my own word — and to me my word is a holy thing — that what I promise I will give you, and if we make a peace, you and I, it will never be broken by the white man."

He looked piercingly at Cochise. "Let us put the whole history of our warfare behind us. Let us start from a new beginning, with no bad memories. There were mistakes and outrages on both sides. Let us close the book on them

[234]

and hereafter walk together as brothers. And if we are honorable and truthful with each other, then one day there need be no reservations. White men and Indians will trust each other and then all may walk freely and without fear."

Cochise meditated on the words. Then he said to Jeffords: "I think he speaks with a straight tongue, Sheekasay. What do you think?"

Jeffords looked at Howard, at the white beard and the clear eyes. "I think so too," he said.

Howard stood up. He straightened his uniform and squared his tired shoulders. "I will go to Fort Bowie now. I will give the necessary orders. Who among you will come with me?"

Chee stepped forward immediately. "I will go."

Howard put his arm on Chee's shoulder. "Good, my friend. Come with me. We will ride together again."

And then Tahzay stepped forward and he said in a quiet voice: "I too would like to ride with the American *nantan*."

Cochise's eyes widened.

General Howard lifted his head and his eyes sparkled. "The son of Cochise and the son of Mangas Coloradas! Surely this proves that Almighty God is on the side of my mission!"

CHAPTER XXIII

Late the following afternoon a small band of Apache warriors whipped their flagging ponies up the trail to the Stronghold. The leader reported to Cochise that they had had a running fight with a scouting party of soldiers from Fort Bowie, and that after killing several of the soldiers, they had managed to escape from the rest.

Cochise called Jeffords and Captain Sladen to his side and said: "I do not think the soldiers can follow the trail of my Indians, but if they do we will have a fight."

Jeffords translated the statement of the Indian to the American captain. "If the troops do find this place, they will be defeated, Captain," he said. "If you want to leave, you had better go right away. I'll get one of the Indians to take you to General Howard."

The young captain replied: "What are you going to do, Mr. Jeffords?"

"I'm going to stay here," Jeffords replied. "But you're an army officer. It might complicate things if soldiers discovered you were on this side of the battle line."

Sladen said: "If you are going to stay — I'll stay too."

Jeffords clapped the captain heartily on the shoulder. "All right, Captain," he said. "Keep your eyes open. You'll learn a few things."

Captain Sladen watched Cochise set about preparing for the defense of the Stronghold. The Chiricahua leader took advantage of every natural protection of the great open amphitheater. Men were stationed so that their field of fire covered every approach to the Stronghold. Women were sent to the rear of the Stronghold so they could move out easily to another secret camp if the soldiers were able to force their way into the rancheria.

When Cochise finished with his preparations, Sladen turned to Jeffords and said: "I would hate to be the commander of any force ordered to try to break in here, Mr. Jeffords. I think I would need an entire army to breach these defenses."

In the night, after supper, Jeffords and Sladen spread their blankets and lay down under the brilliant, starry sky. Presently Cochise joined them. The Indian and Jeffords spoke to each other for a long time, recalling old events, and then Cochise said: "It may be that the long trail of war has come to an end at last, Sheekasay. I have faith in this general — because of you."

"I may be wrong, my brother," Jeffords said.

Cochise shook his head. "No, since he came with you it must be good. It was not intended that you were to become my brother only to bring treachery to us. Your general speaks much of his God. The Indian has a God too. Maybe the two Gods arranged all this."

Jeffords smiled. "It may be, Cochise."

"The most important thing is that you have tried to do good for us, Sheekasay. If it proves bad — it also proves what I said long ago: we are above our own people."

The Indians maintained a vigil during the night, but the American soldiers never appeared. General Howard returned to the rancheria the following afternoon. He had ridden through the night and had accomplished his mission at Fort Bowie with great speed and had returned without resting.

When he entered the camp he noticed the defensive measures instantly and Jeffords explained to him why they had been taken. Howard's trained military eye took in every detail of Cochise's planning and then he said with profound respect to the Indian chief: "Cochise, no general in the United States Army could have made a better disposition of his men to resist an attack from an enemy force."

Cochise received the compliment proudly. "I have had to learn these things a hard way," he said.

The peace conference was to be held in the West Stronghold. Cochise led the Americans there. Howard gazed around him in awe. He said: "I thought your other camp offered a perfect place for defense. It is nothing to what you have here. Cochise, God did not intend for you to be defeated in battle!"

"Your God or mine?" Cochise asked.

Howard's Biblical face became stern. "There is but one God, Cochise. All creatures are His children."

"That is something God may know," Cochise replied. "His children know it not."

The Indians celebrated the return of General Howard from Fort Bowie and the beginning of the peace talks with a dance. Jeffords and Captain Sladen went to a mound of stones and set up a white flag. The women shrieked their approval and repeated a long Apache word over and over again.

"What are they saying?" Howard asked Jeffords.

"They say: 'The flag of peace I love,'" Jeffords said.

Howard knelt and bowed his head. When he rose his face showed a radiant hope.

Cochise provided a comfortable wickiup for Howard and Sladen and gave them an old Apache woman to serve them as housekeeper. When the general and his aide were rested, they left the dwelling and joined the festive people. The women immediately besought them to dance.

"Go ahead," Jeffords said to Howard. "Everything that you do now will be important."

"It is an easy thing to do, Mr. Jeffords — to dance with these people," Howard replied. "They are good."

The two American officers entered into the dancing circle. One girl held to Howard's left hand and another grasped his empty right sleeve. Howard kicked out his legs like any young buck. Sladen found himself between two attractive Indian girls and he smiled from ear to ear as he bounded to and from the fire.

Jeffords and Cochise, sitting side by side, looked on and smiled. After the dancing there was the usual feast. The celebration lasted almost through the night.

Daily the warriors returned to the Stronghold in little bands from their expeditions throughout the country. Howard, filled with calm serenity, prayed frequently, and it soon was whispered among the people that he was some kind of holy man.

He walked around the camp, looking at all the phases of domestic Apache life with vast interest, his kindliness trailing after him. He watched women at work and children at play and he always had several of the younger children following him. He kept a diary of his days in the camp and when he sat down to write the children clustered around him.

One afternoon he taught Nachise, younger son of Cochise, to write his name. The other children were fascinated. He asked each of them to say his own name slowly and then he wrote it down. The children were delighted and they, in their turn, tried to teach the old general simple Apache words, and they chortled over his pronunciation.

When all the warriors and lesser chiefs were finally gathered together, Cochise assembled them and then sent for the Americans. In the presence of Howard, Cochise told his warriors how the American general had come to him from the American *nantan* in Washington, asking for a peace to end the long war.

Cochise said to Howard: "We will talk about this. But we must be allowed to remain in our own country. These mountains have been our home for as long as there is any memory in our people. We will not be moved elsewhere."

"It will be as you say," Howard replied quietly.

Howard listened as each Apache fighting man spoke his piece. It appeared to him to be an example of democracy in action — not much different from the town meetings of the Americans, where each person, regardless of his position, had a right to make himself heard.

Although Howard could not tell what the men were saying, except when Jeffords translated for him, he soon realized that there was a conflict of opinion. Some of the warriors appeared to desire peace. Others bitterly opposed it, maintaining that the word of the white man could not be relied upon.

Through all the discussion, Cochise sat with a set expression on his face. He listened each man out and did not attempt to argue with him.

In the evening the Indians moved to a high plateau a quarter of a mile from where the first council was held. This time the white men were ordered to remain behind.

"What are they doing up there?" Howard asked Jeffords anxiously.

Jeffords's eyes were blue and unwinking. "They are having a prayer meeting, General."

"A prayer meeting?"

"They are up there consulting their God," Jeffords said. "They are telling Him what you offered and they are waiting for a sign."

"May I go and join them?"

"No, General, this is something between the Indians and their own Maker. They'll come down and tell us whether they want to make a peace or not."

Howard sat down on a rock. "Then there is nothing to do but wait, Mr. Jeffords," he said quietly. "I too can tell my Maker what has been offered. In His wisdom and mercy He surely is on the side of peace."

"I'm glad that you don't think that what they are doing up there is funny, General," Jeffords said.

Howard looked at him gently. "What can be funny about a man asking God for guidance, Mr. Jeffords?"

He removed his hat and got down on his knees. Then Jeffords did a strange thing. He knelt beside the old man and bowed his own head and although he had no words from the Bible to say, he too asked God that the verdict might be peace.

The three white men sat in a long unbroken silence. From off in the distance they heard the muffled sound of many voices. The women moaned in unison as though imitating the rising and the falling of the wind. Then the men's voices joined them and together the two sets of sounds rose higher and higher, filling the air.

Sladen stared ahead of him. Howard read from his Bible. Jeffords smoked and listened and lost himself in his thoughts.

Then Tahzay appeared. His long hair hung behind his neck. His face was covered with paint. He appeared suddenly and with violence and Jeffords thought at that moment how much he was like Cochise and how fortunate the Apache people were to have him to follow his father.

When Tahzay spoke his voice was gentle: "You will all come and join us," he said.

The three men followed him. When they reached the plateau they found the warriors seated in a circle, and around them in a larger circle were the women. Tahzay pointed to a place and the three Americans sat down.

The singing and the prayer now were ended. Cochise spoke. He spoke with his arms uplifted and his head raised and General Howard thought then that he had never before seen so noble and impressive a man. Howard heard his name repeated again and again as Cochise addressed his people. He also heard the word "Sheekasay" uttered repeatedly, and he knew that Cochise was emphasizing that this envoy for peace had been brought to the Apaches by their old and trusted friend, Thomas Jeffords.

When Cochise finished he beckoned to General Howard. The general rose and walked to the side of the Apache chief. Cochise placed his hand on Howard's shoulder. He said: "Hereafter the white man and the Indian are to drink of the same water, eat of the same bread, and be at peace. I pledge this."

Then Tahzay said: "As the son of Cochise, I pledge this."

Jeffords translated the words to Howard. The old general lifted his face to the sky and he said: "I thank Thee, O my God, for having given my mission success."

On a flat rock, Captain Sladen spread out a map he had taken from his pouch. From it, General Howard outlined the boundaries of the new Chiricahua Apache Reservation, which included all the traditional hunting lands of the tribe. Jeffords went over the map carefully, and assured Cochise that the boundaries were fair and just.

Cochise placed his hand on the map and agreed to its borders. He said: "There is one more condition."

"What is that?" General Howard asked.

"Sheekasay must be Indian Agent."

Jeffords started to translate the words and then stopped abruptly. "What!" he exclaimed.

"What is he saying?" Howard asked.

"Yes," Jeffords said to Cochise. "What are you saying?"

"What is he saying, Mr. Jeffords?" Howard repeated.

"He says that *I* must be Indian Agent," Jeffords said.

"Excellent!" Howard cried. "I cannot conceive of a better choice."

"Nothing doing," Jeffords said. Then he said to Cochise: "It is not for me."

"We will make peace," Cochise said. "All cattle and horses we have taken from the whites will be returned. The

Indians will live at peace — but Sheekasay must be our agent."

"I do not want the job," Jeffords said.

"Then the peace talk is ended," Cochise said.

"Unless you consent to act as Indian Agent I cannot make the peace," Howard said. "You must understand what your refusal means, Mr. Jeffords."

Jeffords was still looking at his old friend. Cochise was without expression, but then Jeffords saw the faint glint of amusement in his eyes. "All right," Jeffords said. "I'll take the job."

"It is yours," Howard said. "In the name of the President of the United States, I appoint you Agent for the Chiricahua Reservation."

Now Cochise embraced his blood brother. "It is good."

"How long have you planned this?" Jeffords asked him.

"The arrow of war now is broken," Cochise said.

"How long have you planned this?"

Cochise smiled. "It is better that you stay with us. You are more Indian than I am. We will watch out for you so that nothing happens to you."

He put his arm around his son. "More and more Tahzay is learning to be leader. There will be no more fighting. I will have little to do." He looked at Jeffords and his lined, worn face was serene. "Sheekasay," he said, "the days will be long. I want somebody to talk to."

The sun was high over the Stronghold. The war arrow was broken. The terrible mistake that had been made many years before by a thoughtless young officer now was corrected. From then on, the dreaded Chiricahua Apaches lived at peace with the white men; and in the long days and the long evenings, the two men who had crossed all lines of race to become blood brothers spoke of the things they had seen and done. And the land was at peace.